A PASSAGE OF THREATS

A SHADE OF VAMPIRE 47

BELLA FORREST

ALSO BY BELLA FORREST

A Shade of Vampire (Book 1)

A Shade of Blood (Book 2)

A Castle of Sand (Book 3)

A Shadow of Light (Book 4)

A Blaze of Sun (Book 5)

A Gate of Night (Book 6)

A Break of Day (Book 7)

Series 2: Rose & Caleb's story

A Shade of Novak (Book 8)

A Bond of Blood (Book 9)

A Spell of Time (Book 10)

A Chase of Prey (Book 11)

A Shade of Doubt (Book 12)

A Turn of Tides (Book 13)

A Dawn of Strength (Book 14)

A Fall of Secrets (Book 15)

An End of Night (Book 16)

Series 3: The Shade continues with a new hero...

A Wind of Change (Book 17)

A Trail of Echoes (Book 18)

A Soldier of Shadows (Book 19)

A Hero of Realms (Book 20)

A Tide of War (Book 41)

Series 6: A Gift of Three

A Gift of Three (Book 42)

A House of Mysteries (Book 43)

A Tangle of Hearts (Book 44)

A Meet of Tribes (Book 45)

A Ride of Peril (Book 46)

A Passage of Threats (Book 47)

A SHADE OF DRAGON TRILOGY

A Shade of Dragon 1

A Shade of Dragon 2

A Shade of Dragon 3

A SHADE OF KIEV TRILOGY

A Shade of Kiev 1

A Shade of Kiev 2

A Shade of Kiev 3

BEAUTIFUL MONSTER DUOLOGY

Beautiful Monster 1

Beautiful Monster 2

DETECTIVE ERIN BOND (Adult thriller/mystery)

Lights, Camera, GONE

Write, Edit, KILL

For an updated list of Bella's books, please visit her website: www.bellaforrest.net

Join Bella's VIP email list and she'll personally send you an email reminder as soon as her next book is out. Sign up: www.forrestbooks.com

NEW GENERATION LIST

- **Aida:** daughter of Bastien and Victoria (half werewolf/half human)
- **Field:** biological son of River, adopted son of Benjamin (mix of Hawk and vampire-half-blood)
- **Jovi:** son of Bastien and Victoria (half werewolf/half human)
- **Phoenix:** son of Hazel and Tejus (sentry)
- **Serena:** daughter of Hazel and Tejus (sentry)
- **Vita:** daughter of Grace and Lawrence (part-fae/human)

1

SERENA

It did not look good. We all stood outside the mansion beneath the protective shield, as dozens of Destroyers and swarms of Azazel's green fireflies circled the property. The fact that they were unable to see or hear through the Daughters' spell was the only thing that helped me keep it together, and, judging by the looks on the others' faces, it was a collective thought.

"We can't stay here forever. That much is clear," Jovi muttered.

He paced around the group, looking at the monsters waiting outside. Knowing him, he was scanning them for potential weak spots. After all, how often did we get the chance to stare the enemy in the face without getting killed?

Aida and Field stood close to each other. The Hawk looked sullen as he occasionally glanced at the squished fireflies in the grass at his feet, scattered between pieces of broken glass. I couldn't help but sympathize with his misery. He couldn't have known what those little bastards were. He'd only tried to do something nice for Aida.

Vita seemed pale.

Bijarki inched closer to her. The moment their eyes met, some of the tension seemed to leave her petite frame. She looked to the side and frowned as one Destroyer, the one named Goren, took another step forward, bumping into the invisible shield.

Sverik blanched. I couldn't blame him. We'd just rescued him from something akin to hell, and now he was stuck here, surrounded by the very demons he'd narrowly managed to escape.

Draven stood next to me, his expression alternating between pensive and infuriated, a deep crease drawing a dark shadow between his eyebrows.

We'd briefly gone over options, and venturing through the passage stone beneath the mansion had seemed like the most viable one—although it was challenging and risky.

"What about the invisibility spell?" I asked, wishing there was another way. "We could use it to leave, a few of us. It will hold us for at least a mile, based on our previous experience, and it should be enough to get out of here unseen and get help from Sverik's incubi brethren and the Dearghs."

"There isn't enough," Draven replied. "We need to use what we have left wisely and only in the absence of other choices. It will take months for some of the plants needed to grow back. We've used up the existing supply, and they can't be found anywhere nearby."

It seemed like all our roads led to the passage stone below.

"Come out, come out, whoever you are," Goren bawled from the jungle beyond the shield.

He took one of his swords out and used it to scratch the surface of the spell as he walked along its border, leaving a shower of golden sparks behind. It sounded like metal screeching against metal, but that was all it could do—make noise.

Anjani and Hansa watched him, their eyes glinting and their mouths twisted with fury and disgust, as if they were watching the world's largest cockroach parading through a fine fruit cake.

Hansa was the first to react. I heard the whistling sound of her sword leaving its scabbard as she charged toward Goren, eager to slice him up.

"By the Daughters, I will chop you into pieces and—"

She didn't get far. Sverik grabbed Hansa from behind, wrapping his arms around her waist as he lifted her off the ground. The succubus was strong even for him. Sverik struggled with her before Bijarki jumped in to help calm her down.

Her arms and legs flailed, and she roared for the Destroyer's head.

"Let me go!" she barked. "He killed my sisters, my daughters, my friends! Let me go! I need to do this!"

"You'll do it another time, Hansa!" Bijarki shouted as he helped Sverik bring her back to our group.

She didn't stop struggling, though, and made it extremely difficult for the two army-trained incubi to keep her from darting back toward Goren.

"Let me go! I have to wipe that smirk off his putrid face!" she heaved.

They put her down but held her arms behind her back.

"You'll expose us all," Sverik pleaded. "We have to be smart about this!"

Finally, she conceded defeat and accepted Sverik and Bijarki's line of reasoning. I glanced over at Anjani and wasn't surprised to see the genetic similarity to Hansa. Unlike her sister, however, the young succubus seemed to have a slower reaction time and no use for words.

She slipped away from the group, pulling both knives from her belt as she ran toward the shield. Her expression spelled a most painful death.

"Anjani, no!" I shouted, enough to catch Jovi's attention.

She was fast but not as fast as Jovi, who shot across the grass and swept her off her feet, inches from the protective shield and Goren's disgusting grin.

"Please, don't do this," Jovi said to Anjani as he carried her back to us.

She didn't say anything, gritting her teeth and breathing heavily as tears glazed her eyes. She looked at him for a moment before she sighed and shuddered, breathing in and out in an attempt to regain her composure as Jovi put her down.

"You will both get your revenge against Goren and every other creature responsible for your sisters' deaths. I promise you that," Draven said solemnly. "But for now, we need to focus on what lies ahead and what needs to be done."

"Easy for you to say," Tamara the Lamia screeched, visibly infuriated. "You're probably used to these slithering monsters roaming around, but you've put my daughter and me in danger! What sort of alliance do you wish to achieve here, when you put our heads in the snake's mouth?"

Her daughter, Eva, didn't seem as upset, but fear flickered in her amber eyes. She stayed quiet, occasionally glancing at Draven as her mother continued her rant.

"I didn't come all the way here to get torn apart by these oversized snakes! I came here for an alliance, for a peaceful talk with a Druid! Get us out of here now! It is your duty!"

Draven raised his voice to the volume of thunder. "Will you please just shut up? I obviously did not plan for this to happen, and your hysteria isn't helping. If anything, it's distracting. So please, let me think."

Tamara's eyes widened, and her mouth shrank into a thin red line on her alabaster face. Her nostrils flared with indignation, but she kept her mouth shut.

"We could just shift into snakes and try to get out," Eva mumbled mostly to herself.

"I'm not putting you in such danger unless we have to. This is the Druid's doing, he must fix it!" Tamara snapped.

"Please, be quiet for a second," Draven hissed.

Perhaps it wasn't polite of him, but she'd had it coming. I would've said worse, particularly after her alliance conditions regarding the impregnation of her daughter by Draven.

A moment passed before Draven spoke again.

The rest of us watched the massive Destroyers walk along the edge. They used their weapons to charge the shield head on and failed miserably each time.

"As you can all see, the Daughters' magic is impenetrable, otherwise the Destroyers would already be inside," Draven said. "You should all be safe here while we attempt to get out through the passage stone. We cannot all stay here and wait for the problem to solve itself. Risks must be taken or we all perish here in the end."

"Who are you referring to when you say 'we attempt to get out'?" Field asked.

"I know I have no way of convincing Serena to sit this one out," he replied. "And given that she's proven herself an invaluable asset to this campaign, I'd be foolish not to ask her to come with me."

Draven looked at me as he said those words. His look warmed my insides, and my heart swelled with pride.

"Hansa should join us as well," he continued. "Her skills are of more use on the outside, rather than sulking in here." He looked at her and smiled briefly, enough to make her understand that she was valued and that he wasn't ready to lose her to a botched attempt at revenge against Goren. "Sverik will come as well, since he knows where the incubi outpost is. Something tells me he'd rather land in a volcano via the passage stone than stay here, surrounded by the very beasts who caged him."

"Not to be a buzzkill, but the protective shield sounds better than hot, burning lava," Sverik smirked. "Nevertheless, I will gladly join you on this mission, not only because you need my guidance to find the rogues, but also because I cannot stay here while my rescuers face countless other dangers to save this world."

Draven nodded and looked at all of us, trying to give us a reassuring smile. The corners of his mouth struggled to lift.

"Let us go inside the banquet hall and get everything ready," he said. "We leave in a few hours, and there is no time to waste. We have to cover all possible scenarios with what we do next, as there is the risk of Vita's vision coming to fruition, while we still have a lot of work to do and ground to cover."

2

SERENA

"What do you want the rest of us to do?" Phoenix asked as soon as we entered the banquet hall.

"First and foremost, we need the Daughter to take the swamp witches' book and translate anything that may be of use to us on this mission," Draven replied and took his seat at the head of the table.

"We don't know what will be waiting for us on the other side," Hansa said to the Daughter, who stood quietly by my brother's side. "We don't know where the other passage stones are. Our worst-case scenarios involve getting trapped beneath several feet of dirt, falling into a volcano, drowning, or, Daughters forbid, walking right into Azazel's chamber, where my passage stone probably is by now. We will need any spell that can help with protection from such calamities, as well as combat magic if you can find any. Whatever you can dig up in the next two to three hours, we'll take it."

The Daughter nodded firmly and left the hall to fetch the spell book.

Phoenix sat down across from Aida and poured himself a glass of water. I could see a muscle jerking in his jaw, a sign of tension I'd rarely seen in him.

My heart got smaller with each minute that passed, as my brain processed all the risks involved—each ending with me never seeing Phoenix, my friends, and my family again. Then again, there was the slim chance we'd make it safely out of here and do what we'd set out to do. I channeled all my energy into that one positive outcome. I figured that the universe would be more tempted to work in my favor if I focused on the most positive, if unlikely, scenario.

"Anjani," Draven said, "I need you to check all our supplies, from herbs to powders, potions, and poisons. Anything we can carry in the satchels, we'll take them. We have to be prepared for any hostile creature we might come across, Sluaghs included. So, don't skimp on that death's kiss toxin either."

She nodded and gave Jovi a quick glance before she headed out to the greenhouse. As a succubus of few words, I figured it was her way of saying, "See you later." With the dangers waiting outside, every gesture counted.

Aida, Vita, and Field sat next to each other. Bijarki and Sverik hovered nearby, occasionally glancing at the two Lamias who'd found seats at the other end of the table.

"What can I do?" Bijarki asked, hands in his pockets.

"Can you get some weapons ready? Something light that we can easily carry. We don't need anything that will weigh us down, should we find ourselves in the middle of a lake or an ocean," Draven replied.

"What about us?" Aida looked at me.

"We need your visions," I replied. "Everything you've seen so far, every detail you can remember."

"I've made notes of their runes during the visions, as well," Field added. "But the Daughter has yet to translate them. They're very recent."

"The swamp witches' spells are a priority right now," Draven replied. "Should the Daughter manage to translate the runes before we leave as well, good. If not, they'll have to wait until we get back."

"Is there anything I can do?" Field asked.

Draven shook his head. "Nothing other than watching over the Oracles. We need you here, since you are one of the strongest and your wings might come in handy. Although, personally, I'm hoping you won't need them while we're away."

I could tell from the look in Field's eyes that he still battled his guilt. I wanted to say something to soothe him, but as soon as Aida leaned against his shoulder, I watched him relax a little. It was enough for me to understand that she had a calming effect on him. We needed him sharp and strong. There was no room for unnecessary guilt clouding his judgment. Our Hawk was strong and fierce and unyielding, and we couldn't have it any other way.

3

VITA

Jovi continued pacing the room like he'd done outside, constantly looking through the window. I craned my neck to get a glimpse of what he was seeing, and another wave of chills shot through me. Destroyers were very much still there, beyond the shield, prowling like bloodthirsty predators trying to get in. It was a shame that the shape-shifters were smaller in size and not strong enough to take on the Destroyers, I would've enjoyed that show.

Phoenix was the first to describe his visions. I registered a slight tremor in his voice as he spoke—he was as rattled as Aida and I were.

"The visions came to me in a set of three again," he said, his finger drawing invisible circles on the table. "I saw a massive hall with a big banquet table in the middle that held twenty seats. It was surrounded by twenty different doors carved into the circular wall, and each led to one of Eritopia's planets. From what I could tell, they were like portals."

"That was the Grand Council Hall you've just described," Draven replied. "It was where the Druid leaders of Eritopia's twenty planets once met on a regular basis to discuss state affairs. I don't know what happened to it. The magic that held it together was extremely powerful, created by the first rulers. It could only be reached through those doors, one on each planet, their locations undisclosed. Only the Druid in charge and his predecessors knew where they were."

"I saw Almus there, along with your mother, Genevieve."

At the sound of her name, Draven's expression softened, a glimmer of sadness temporarily flickering in his gray eyes. He'd never met her, but the longing he must've felt was entirely understandable. I didn't know where I'd be if I hadn't had my mother in my life.

"And I saw Azazel there, before he became a Destroyer," Phoenix continued. "I saw their tattoos, the circles. Their arms were covered with them."

"Druids earn an arm ring tattoo for each completed stage of their apprenticeship," Draven explained. "Our education comes in levels. When all ninety-nine stages are completed, Druids can ascend to a leadership position, and only then do they receive the very last tattoo, the hundredth, on their upper left shoulder. It's a tradition of sorts, marking the hierarchy among our kind."

"So, your mother and father each ruled over a planet?" I asked.

Draven nodded.

"My father had the seventh kingdom, the smallest of Eritopia's planets, but crucial to our world. It held the Druid Academy, where seasoned scholars taught the magic arts to young Druids. It's where they got their ninety-nine tattoos after centuries of study and practice. It was a place of knowledge and mysticism, where the laws of physics were bent by the will of the Druids. Nothing was as it seemed there. Nothing did what it should. Azazel might own it now, but I have a hard time believing he can actually control it. Millennia of wisdom has been stored in that place, most of it long before Azazel was even born."

"What about your mother?" Serena chimed in. "Which planet did she rule over?"

He looked at her and smiled. "This one right here. You might find it wild and unwelcoming, but it wasn't always like this. It's the biggest in Eritopia and filled with precious resources. Over half of its wealth came from exports alone, as it sustained the other planets."

"So your mother was quite powerful," I concluded.

"Indeed, she was. It's why it took Azazel a long time to overthrow the Council, as his kingdom depended on her resources."

"He didn't seem so murderous during this Council meeting," Phoenix continued. "He was friendly and eager to talk, but he was irritated with the bureaucracy. He'd made changes to his military at the time, and the Council, which hadn't been consulted about the changes, ultimately overthrew his decision. It pissed him off big time."

"That doesn't come as a shock. The Council's old-fashioned way of doing things through a string of approvals was one of the main reasons behind his bloody rebellion," Draven mused.

"In the second vision, I saw him watching Almus and Genevieve from afar. I believe your parents were getting to know each other better at the time." Phoenix grinned.

The Druid's eyes flickered black for a second, as he took a deep breath and waited patiently for Phoenix to continue his account.

"It's in this vision that I saw him meet Tamara," he added, glancing over at the Lamia, whose face lit up at the sound of her name. "No one knew she was a Lamia at the time."

"You have to admit, I'm as beautiful now as I was then, right?" Tamara quipped.

Phoenix cocked his head to one side, his grimace disagreeing. It prompted the Lamia to scoff and lean back against her chair, arms crossed.

"That's just your opinion," she replied, clearly irritated. "Besides, it isn't true. Genevieve knew exactly what I was when she took me in, like I've said before."

"But Azazel didn't know," Phoenix shot back, and she stiffened. He then focused his attention on Draven. "Azazel was in love with your mother, Druid. I could see it in his eyes, the longing, the frustration, and the anger at the sight of Almus holding her hand. But when Tamara showed up, he fell for her. I'm guessing he'd been trying to resign himself to the idea that Genevieve and Almus would never separate, that he would never get a chance to be with her, so when the Lamia entered his life, he channeled his love toward her."

A moment passed before Phoenix spoke again, as the new information sank in. I had a hard time imagining Azazel as anything other than the slithering abomination that I'd seen in my visions. I couldn't see him falling in love or yearning for someone to love him back.

"My third vision took me to Azazel after he became a Destroyer, most likely right after he started tearing down Eritopia's leadership system. He'd killed at least some of the other Druids for sure, and he'd begun collecting Oracles already. He was taunting one for information about Tamara, who had run off, pregnant with his child."

"That child was me," Eva interjected.

Judging by the tone of her voice, her paternal heritage wasn't something she was particularly proud of.

Phoenix nodded in response. "He was desperate to find you and your mother, but the Oracle refused to help him. Given that you're both here with us today, I'll go ahead and assume he never found you."

Draven sighed, then looked at Aida. "What can you tell us, wolf-girl?"

Aida straightened her back and cleared her throat, glancing out the window with a frown.

"I saw Azazel in his chamber, conferring with two of his top lieutenants, Goren and Patrik," she replied, prompting Hansa to groan and look out the window. "They were talking about Roderick's clan not having sworn fealty to Azazel yet."

"I know Roderick," Sverik interjected. "He's a good man, from my father's generation. He's one of the last still standing against Azazel. His armed forces are not to be played with."

"Which is probably why Azazel hasn't simply wiped them off the face of this planet," Aida continued. "He needs the armies, from what I understand. Patrik persuaded Azazel to hold off on doing things his bloody way, saying he's close to convincing Roderick to join on his own. They then talked about Marchosi, his latest catch. He's turning into a Destroyer now, but the others don't seem to trust him much. What I can tell you for sure is that becoming a Destroyer isn't necessarily a choice. Azazel described the process briefly, and it seems to me that his dark magic is at the core, infecting Druids like a disease, ultimately dismantling their will. When the transformation is complete, the Destroyer's body and will belong to Azazel, and they can do nothing against it."

"So, what you're saying is that there's a chance that most of these Destroyers didn't exactly choose to become what they are today?" Serena asked.

"Yes. Once they surrender to Azazel, he does something to them. I think he needs them to comply first, to willingly give in to him, before his magic can take over. From my visions, I can tell you for a fact that Marchosi is still struggling with his transformation. I think he only told Azazel he'd help him to escape torture. And Patrik struggled as well at first. According to Goren, he fought long and hard against his condition, constantly trying to get back to Almus somehow."

"Patrik was one of my father's generals," Draven explained. "I never met him, but my father only had good things to say about him. His capture brought much suffering, as Patrik was essential to my father's plans to counteract Azazel's toxic expansion."

"It's interesting to note that Patrik and Goren don't like each other very much," Aida replied. "There is tension between them, as Goren is willfully loyal while Patrik has no choice, since Azazel's magic compels him."

The Druid nodded. "That is very good to know, indeed."

Aida then looked at Hansa and smiled gently. "There are succubi from your tribe who survived," she said.

Hansa lit up, a glimmer of hope rippling through her emerald-gold eyes.

"You saw them?" she gasped.

"Yes. They were camping somewhere in the forests nearby. There are twelve of them, of which two are very young. They sat around a fire, discussing their next steps. They agreed to go back to the camp and see if anyone else survived. They used something called prayer dust," Aida recalled.

"Smart girls!" Hansa grinned. "What happened when they used it?"

"The fire burst violet, and a tear-shaped diamond appeared

beneath the embers with a flame inside."

Hansa leaned back against her chair, nonplussed. She looked at Draven. "The Daughters answered a prayer," she said.

"What's prayer dust?" I asked.

"It's a rare powder. It can no longer be found anywhere. A few grams were left here and there with the succubi tribes after Azazel started killing left and right. No one knows how to make it, but it's part of ancient prayer rituals known to effectively reach out to the Daughters," Hansa explained. "We had very little left ourselves. I kept it hidden in my tent. The girls must have taken it during the attack."

A long minute went by before Draven beckoned Aida to continue her account with a brief nod.

"My third vision took me to Jovi, Anjani, and Bijarki, as they rode their horses toward the River Pyros. They were being followed by rogue incubi."

"Yeah, they chased us for a while and attacked," Jovi confirmed. "But Lamias came out of nowhere and helped us capture two of them. The incubi were rogues looking to cash in on a ransom. We left them with the Lamias."

"Ah yes, the triplets." Tamara grinned. "They're scouts. They keep the scoundrels away, especially those venturing out from the Sarang Marketplace. They're not to be played with. I've trained them well."

"What ransom?" Draven asked, clearly uninterested in the Lamias' prowess.

It occurred to me that the animosity between Druids and

Lamias ran deep, the result of millennia of separation and disdain.

"There's a price on my head," Bijarki replied. "Azazel knows I'm involved in the rebellion against him. He's spread the word."

My heart jumped at the statement. Then it shrank into a frozen ball inside my chest.

"Well, that doesn't help," the Druid murmured. "It means you need to keep away from crowded places where you could be recognized."

"Well, it's not like I'm in a rush to go anywhere right now, given our current circumstances." Bijarki shrugged, a bitter smirk tugging at the corner of his mouth.

It was my turn to speak. I took a deep breath, ignoring the chills running through my veins as I remembered everything I'd seen during my visions. It was time to tell them about Jovi—I could no longer postpone it.

"I had three visions as well," I started. "First, it was a snippet of the near future, from what I could tell. Marchosi was with Goren and Patrik, still struggling with his condition. They both urged him to stop fighting it, as it would ease the pain. Azazel's spell will take over sooner or later, but the process is longer and much more painful if you resist it."

"So, if you give into it, it takes over smoothly," Draven concluded, and I nodded in response.

"There's something I didn't tell you guys," I breathed out with a shudder. "One of my first visions from the future had us Oracles captured by Azazel, somewhere at the top of his castle."

I looked around the table, registering the shock and gloom that took over my friends, one after another. It was too late to turn back now. I had to tell them the whole story.

"That wasn't the worst part," I continued. "In that vision, Jovi is killed by a Destroyer's spear."

Aida's face dropped. Her gaze darted toward Jovi, who sat motionless, eyes wide open as he watched me tell him about his future death. My heart broke, but at least now that he knew, we could work together and find a way to stop it from happening.

"But then, that vision changed. During this recent set of three, I saw a different outcome. There was a siege on Azazel's castle, led by Hansa and Anjani, from what I could tell. Dearghs, succubi, Lamias, and even incubi and other rogues came together and fought hard against the Destroyers and incubi armies loyal to Azazel. Then, there was a massive explosion at the top of his castle. A bright pink flash swallowed it before it all crumbled before my eyes. I saw Anjani cry out Jovi's name, looking up at the explosion. Jovi was up there when it ripped through the castle."

A moment passed in utter silence as we all looked at each other. My stomach churned. I wasn't done with the bad news yet. I swallowed back tears, willing myself to keep my cool and not collapse in front of the people I loved.

"So, I still die," Jovi concluded, his voice low.

"No, that can't be. No, just no!" Aida murmured, her entire body trembling as fear settled on her features.

Jovi stood up and went over to her. He squeezed her shoulders and dropped a kiss on her forehead, as she sniffed and continuously shook her head.

"It's okay, Aida. It'll be okay," he mumbled.

"No, Jovi, it's not okay. I am not letting you die. I am not losing you!" she nearly shouted.

I nodded, unable to hold the tears back anymore. My eyes stung, and I felt the hot streams down my cheeks.

"I'm sorry, Jovi," I managed to say.

He gave me a weak smile, sadness in his eyes.

"It's not your fault, Vita. There's nothing to be sorry about," he replied.

"I should have told you sooner."

"It's okay. I would've had a hard time saying that kind of stuff if I were in your shoes. Really, it's okay."

"And you know by now that they will make it inside the shield at some point," I sobbed. "My third vision took me to a room here in the mansion, in the middle of the night. Destroyers crash through it, and I'm captured. They will make it past the shield somehow. I've seen it before, but I thought it was just a bad dream. This time it was clear. I was perfectly awake when I saw it. They will come for me."

My body shuddered as the scene replayed itself in the back of my head, over and over again. Each time, I was knocked out and abducted. Each time, my heart pounded in my chest as I tried to adjust to the idea that eventually I'd be taken by Destroyers. I just couldn't accept it.

4

JOVI

I thought the idea of me dying was the worst I'd hear from Vita's visions, but the notion of Destroyers making it past the protective shield took the grand prize in this whole mess. I felt the chill running through my veins, and, judging by the consternation on everyone else's faces, they were experiencing the same shock.

It felt as though the air had been kicked out of my lungs.

"Destroyers will come in here..." Serena mumbled, as if repeating the words to believe it.

I couldn't blame her. I found it just as hard to believe, but given Vita's visions, I had no other choice but to see it as a possibility.

"How can that be?" Draven replied. "The Daughters' magic cannot be breached by Destroyers or any of Azazel's magic. What you're saying is virtually impossible. Unless it has to do with a previous vision of yours, where Azazel told Serena that the Daughters were gone..."

"And yet I've seen it happen." Vita's voice trembled as she wiped her tears. "They will get through somehow. It could very well be related to the Daughters leaving. It will happen."

"But how?"

"I don't know!" she nearly shouted. "I don't know!"

Bijarki moved to rest his hands on her shoulders, squeezing gently as she took a few deep breaths and closed her eyes. Whatever he did, it worked, as Vita gradually relaxed.

A long moment of silence followed, as we all digested the information we'd been given. I was going to die, and the pain of that thought was impossible to comprehend. My whole body hardened, and a ball of fire grew in my chest and poured through my veins, melting the initial chill until the prospect of my mortality sank in.

My mind wandered back to The Shade. My parents and extended family. My friends. My sister. I'd never see them again. I'd never see Anjani again. The idea drove sharp blades through my throat into my stomach, tearing me apart on the inside. My inner-wolf howled, its echoes rumbling through my head like the sea crashing against a rocky shore.

I'd have to speak to Anjani about all this. She needed to know. We'd come far in a short span of time, and I feared the news of my future death might hurt this fragile thing between us. It was too early in the game for us to say our goodbyes. There was so much left to discover about each other. She rattled me, and I made her glow, and every time I felt her lips on mine, the world around me disappeared.

How could I ever part with that? How could I ever be okay with losing her?

I took a deep breath, trying to tamp down my panic. I was strong. I would find a way out. I would fight, and I would reshape my future. There was too much at stake. Too many moments that I didn't want to miss out on. I longed to discover the million ways I could make Anjani simmer and melt in my arms.

The sound of her calling out my name. The look she gave me when I annoyed her with something trivial. The way her hair fell down her back in a cascade of ink black curls. I didn't want to lose that. No. I would fight.

Once Vita had finished her gut-wrenching revelations, the group scattered around the house—some getting supplies ready for Draven's next mission, while others kept watch of what was going on outside or assisting the incubi in preparing the weapons.

Serena, Draven, and Hansa kept to their side of the table, further discussing mission details, going over every angle in order to increase their chances of survival once they passed through the passage stone.

My future situation made it hard for me to keep a clear

head, so I decided to take it one task at a time. I needed to speak to Anjani first and tell her about Vita's vision before she heard it from anyone else in the house.

I found her in the greenhouse, clipping leaves off a small potted tree. The heat and humidity quickly seeped into my bones, making me break into a sweat. I loosened the top buttons of my shirt as I stepped toward her.

"Can we talk?" I asked.

She looked up at me from her crouched position, then stood to face me.

My stomach felt sour with pain. I looked into her eyes and found it incredibly hard to speak. It took a lot of energy and willpower to tell her something I had trouble saying out loud for myself.

"Vita had a vision of the future," I said.

Anjani was quiet, waiting patiently for me to tell her the whole story. A frown pulled her eyebrows closer together, signaling that she was bracing herself for bad news.

"There will be a siege on Azazel's castle. You and Hansa will be among those leading it. We'll bring an alliance together as we've planned."

She didn't say anything. I had a feeling she knew I wasn't done yet.

"There will be an explosion. I'll be in it," I finally said. "I'm predicted to die."

Anjani was quiet. Her eyes moved, gaze shifting all over my

face. Tears shimmered in the corners of her eyes, and she swallowed them back, her lower lip trembling slightly.

"It's what Vita saw?" she managed to ask.

I nodded slowly.

"I need some air," she said and walked out into the garden.

I followed, unable to say anything else. I watched her as she stepped over the tall grass, looking around. Destroyers kept circling the property while green fireflies flew in thick swarms above. The protective shield glistened gold whenever one of them made contact.

"It's just a probable future, though, isn't it?" she asked, watching Goren in the distance.

"Yes," I replied. "But it's not the first time Vita has seen me die. Before this, she had another vision of a Destroyer killing me. It's not looking all that great from where we stand right now."

"No, Jovi," she said, her voice wavering. "There are millions of possible futures. The one that Vita saw is just one of them. The one most likely to happen. We just have to make sure we avoid it. That's all."

"You make it sound so easy. I like your spirit." I smiled.

"Do I have any other choice?" Anjani turned to face me, and I was stunned.

Her skin glowed an incandescent silver. Powerful emotions moved through her as she looked into my eyes. I felt my chest cave in. I was head over heels with this marvelous creature, and her refusal to accept my fate gave me even more strength to fight whatever was coming to get me.

"I have never allowed fate to bring me to my knees," she said. "If I did, I would have never considered your presence in my life. And yet, here you are, in front of me. My heart tells me that there is no way I will ever allow anyone or anything to take you away from me."

I'd gone through different stages of acknowledging death as a part of my future. I'd experienced pain, sadness, and anger, the latter driving me to find the determination I needed to fight back. The moment I'd laid eyes on Anjani, my resolve had grown even stronger. Just the idea of never seeing her again floored me, but her reaction was truly astounding.

Anjani didn't let death scare her off. It obviously hurt her. I could tell from the way she was glowing that she wasn't taking the news all that well, but at the same time her ability to stand up and tell death, "No, you don't!" made me want to fight with an extra kick in my heel, knowing we'd be in this together.

"Glad to hear you say that." I smiled. "We're on the same page. I'm not ready to say goodbye to you just yet."

Her eyes glimmered as she looked down, glowing even brighter. I'd made her blush again.

"Good, because you won't get rid of me that easily."

My heart stopped.

With a single sentence, Anjani managed to pull me out of my gloom and spark new fires in me. My gaze settled on her lips. I moved to take her in my arms and kiss her and revel in her scent.

Twigs cracked nearby.

Our heads turned simultaneously, watching Hansa as she walked down the front steps of the porch, followed by Sverik. Her hand settled on the hilt of her sword as she reached Goren. She stayed close, inside the shield, but walked along with the Destroyer, who kept sniffing the air with his forked tongue.

"I told you, I won't do anything stupid," Hansa told Sverik as he reached her.

"I can't leave you on your own, Hansa. I'm sorry. There's too much at stake here."

"I'm well aware of that, incubus. That doesn't mean I can't tell this serpent what's waiting for him once I get my hands on him."

We didn't say anything, as Hansa looked at Goren, pointing a finger at his head.

"First, I will peel the skin off his face, to get rid of that disgusting grin of his," she said.

"It's taking her a tremendous amount of self-control to not charge him right now, you know," Anjani murmured, leaning into me.

My hand reached up behind her, finding a good resting spot between her bare shoulder blades. The feel of her skin against my fingertips made my heart flutter, as if nothing could take that feeling away from me. It felt good.

"What about you? I wrestled you away from him once. I don't want to do it again," I quipped.

"You won't. I've made my peace with his death already. His head will roll under Hansa's blade. I'll just slaughter every Sluagh I come across, instead. I'll get my vengeance another way. But Goren is hers, as our leader, our mother, and our sister. I was foolish to attempt anything myself."

"Then I will slice him up, inch by inch, each strip of his filthy flesh will pay for each of my daughters, my sisters, my mothers, and my friends. By the time I'm done with him, he'll be begging for me to kill him," Hansa continued, a few yards away from us.

Goren kept walking, unaware of what was happening just a few inches away from him beyond the shield.

"But I won't kill him. He might pass out from the pain, but I will make sure he stays awake and feels everything. I will burn him alive and watch the flames eat him. I will listen to his screams and wails of death as if enjoying a beautiful song. And when he gives his last breath, when his corpse is charred and lifeless, I will tear it apart and feed it to the worms. Only then will the Red Tribe be avenged."

"Wow, you sound worse than Azazel on a bad day," Sverik replied bluntly. "I thought he had a vivid imagination, but you certainly take the crown on cruelty."

"And he's never seen her actually do such things." Anjani chuckled. "I've seen my sister exact her revenge on others before. Sverik would probably crumble if he could see what she's capable of."

I couldn't blame Hansa when it came to a creature like Goren. All those innocent lives lost, and for what? For a crazy former Druid who was so addicted to power he didn't care how he got it?

Come to think of it, watching Goren as he strode along the shield made me want to rip his head from his neck. But Anjani was right. His death belonged to Hansa.

5

SERENA

I took Draven aside amidst the preparations, as I could no longer stand the angst that Tamara and Eva's presence gave me.

"We need to talk about the Lamias and their alliance condition, Draven," I said with determination.

He took a deep breath and looked to his right. I followed his gaze and saw Tamara and Eva talking by one of the tall French windows of the banquet hall.

"You're right. We can't postpone this conversation any longer," he replied, his voice low. He looked at me. "What are you thinking?"

"What do you mean what am I thinking? What are *you* thinking? Will you accept her terms?"

He shrugged, somehow adding to my aggravation. It was bad enough we had Destroyers stationed outside the shield waiting to kill us all when Vita's vision came true. I didn't have the patience to leave this loose Lamia end lying around for us to trip on later down the line.

"I don't think we have a choice right now," he finally said.

A heavy iron ball dropped inside my stomach. We'd briefly considered this already when Tamara had first mentioned it, but it wasn't any easier to swallow an hour later. I still hated the idea, but we needed the Lamias to fight against Azazel, to increase our chances of survival.

"How will it work, then? You and Eva get busy now or set a date or something? How does it work?" I growled, unable to hide my discomfort.

Draven's eyes lit up, and a grin slit his face.

"Did I ever tell you how brilliant you are, Serena?"

My mind was blocked. I blinked fast several times, trying to process the question. I must've said something that sparked an idea in that twisted Druid head of his that I could no longer live without.

"What do you mean?" I asked.

"Eva and I set a date. We say yes to her proposal but postpone the mating part," he replied. "We'll tell Tamara that Eva and I will mate once the war with Azazel is over. From their perspective, there's no point in making a baby now, anyway. We'll flat out lie."

"That's your solution?"

I failed to see what the brilliant part was, until Draven pointed it out, making me feel silly for a second or two.

"It gives us time to figure out a way to avoid this. Maybe there are other Druids out there still. Maybe we could reverse Azazel's spell on a Destroyer and give Eva another Druid. Maybe Eva won't live to see the end of the war, although that would be a tragedy."

If our situation hadn't been so dire, I would've found his dark humor to be charming. But, given the circumstances, grim giggles were the last thing on my mind. I secretly gave him brownie points for trying.

"Draven, let me be clear," I said. "I will never let you do this for her. Why are they imposing any conditions on us to begin with? They're trapped in here with us, aren't they?"

"Not so much," he replied. "They could transform into serpents and find a way out, although it's extremely dangerous. Tamara wouldn't put the Lamias' lives on the line just for this. If we want them to join willingly, we need to persuade them and we need to appease them. The Lamias don't respond to threats or conditions, they respond to trade. And ultimately, they've been unable to mate with Destroyers. Whatever Azazel did to them, it rendered them sterile, I guess. I really am their last chance at conceiving, at least at this point in time, and believe me when I say that the Lamias place their lineage above everything else."

He came closer, his gaze searching for mine.

"We need to be shrewd and leave our ethics at the door on this one, Serena. We need the Lamias because they are fast, strong, and they have numbers and some minor Druid magic tricks which will come in handy. We need all the help we can get right now. Most importantly, I can convince Tamara that I'll go along with it. But I won't. We lie. Simple as that. We say whatever we need to say to get their allegiance."

"What if this all ends well and Eva expects you to come through?"

"I won't. And Tamara will not go to war over it either. It will just have an impact on my credibility but, by then, Azazel will be gone and I will not care about anything else other than being with you, anyway."

I stared deeply into his gray eyes and found myself ecstatic to be near him, to face all of this with Draven by my side. We made a good team.

"You have a point," I conceded with a dry smile. "We should also consider that there may still be Druids out there, hidden somewhere. We could look for them and convince one of them to take your place in the bargain, once all this is over. Provided I live to see it."

"Don't say that." His gaze darkened. "Of course, you'll live to see it. You and I have a lot to do after we destroy Azazel."."

"Whatever we do, Draven, there is no way in hell I'm letting you anywhere near Eva. She may be quite the babe, but still. No. Just no."

"She's nothing compared to you. I'd rather hug a flaming Deargh than touch her."

In spite of everything, I enjoyed our little back-and-forth

moments. Draven always found a way to knock the air out of my lungs and soften my knees with a well-aimed remark.

"Besides," he added. "Circumstances will most likely change later down the line. For now, even lying is better than the absence of allies."

I nodded in agreement, prompting Draven to take my hand and walk us over to Tamara and Eva. As soon as we reached them, Eva's face lit up, her yellow eyes wide open at the sight of Draven. I would've done anything to wipe that lascivious smile off her face. But my mind shouted the word "alliance" on repeat to keep me in check.

Draven wasted no time in communicating the decision. "We agree to your terms. I will mate with Eva in exchange for your unwavering support against Azazel."

Tamara beamed at us both and tilted her head to one side. "You've made a wise choice, Druid. You have my word. The Lamias will fight for you."

"I do have my own condition to append to this agreement, though," Draven added.

Tamara's smile faded as swiftly as it had appeared, waiting for him to state his terms.

"The mating will happen after we defeat Azazel. There is absolutely no point in bringing a Lamia child into this world when Azazel is out to kill anyone and anything that defies him. You and I both know that your kind is on his death list."

It took her a moment to process the information, but when

it fully registered, her lips pursed. She looked first at her daughter, then at Draven.

"That is fine, Druid. Provided you keep your word and don't backtrack at the last minute," she replied, her tone firm and sharp.

"You have my word, and my word is my bond, Tamara."

A moment passed before either of us said anything. The silence was awkward but understandable—in this agreement, each side had different interests but a common enemy. Eva, however, seemed thrilled by the result. She ran a finger down Draven's chest, fiddling with one of his shirt's buttons.

My blood boiled.

"I guess it'll be you and me later, then." She smiled seductively.

I balled my fists at my sides, trembling in an effort not to smack that smirk off with a carefully launched punch.

"I suggest you wait until after the war is over," I said, gritting my teeth. "Not sure you've noticed, but he is with someone. He'll only be doing you a community service."

"We'll see about that, little girl. No creature has ever resisted my charms." She grinned at me.

"I'm not sure what creature would find you appealing without your hands, because I will chop them off if you don't keep them away from Draven until your term is due."

There was no way for me to back down. I was the stranger, the outsider, in a world that was made up of creatures as wild and beautiful as the very jungles that surrounded them. I couldn't allow myself to come across as weak, especially not in front of a Lamia as brazen as this one.

"You would die before you even think of touching me," Eva hissed.

"Well, at least there would be one person here actually thinking of touching you," I shot back.

She took a step forward, but Tamara's arm stretched out and pushed her back gently, giving both Draven and me a most condescending smirk.

"Now, now, Eva darling, please be mindful of this precious alliance. There is no room for wounded egos in a war against Azazel, so let's be respectful of all those fighting with us," Tamara said in a dry, polite tone. "Even those from the outside who are unlikely to survive."

She looked straight at me.

My blood simmered, and I clenched my teeth, swallowing back a horde of insults. I felt Draven's hand settle on the small of my back, instantly soothing me. She was, after all, due for a major disappointment once this was over. I decided to save my strength for that day, as I considered that I may have to use force to persuade her to drop her mating claim once Draven broke the bad news.

"I suggest you both make yourselves busy elsewhere now, as this conversation is over," he interjected, his voice loaded with ice and contempt.

Tamara shrugged and walked away, followed closely by Eva,

who gave me a death stare over her shoulder before they both left the banquet hall.

Draven pulled me closer, his hand still on my back. He used his index finger and thumb to lift my chin and look me in the eyes. I lost myself in his metallic gaze, and he pressed his lips against mine in a single, most comforting kiss.

"Don't mind them," he whispered. "They're venomous creatures. It's in their nature to be unpleasant."

"I know. They're just making it hard for me to tolerate them on the premises," I mumbled.

"They now know not to mess with you. You've held your ground well. Don't think for a second that a seasoned Lamia like Tamara doesn't appreciate that. She does. She just won't show it." He smiled at me, a hint of pride in his eyes.

My chest felt a little lighter at his words. Not that Tamara's opinion mattered, but I did care what Draven thought. Besides, I wasn't just speaking for myself in this entire campaign against Azazel. I was carrying the Novak torch, and there was no way a young and sharp-tongued Lamia would get the better of me.

6

PHOENIX

The Daughter was busy browsing through spells. I asked Aida to help her write them down. Given everything that had happened, I needed to make sure that Field was all right. The whole green firefly issue had really rattled him. As a promising future leader of GASP, I knew he'd set some high expectations for himself, and bringing Azazel's spies beneath the shield counted as a dismal failure for him. I'd been around him long enough to know what he was thinking.

I looked around for him, eventually climbing up on the rooftop through the attic to find him sitting there quietly, watching Destroyers fly above.

"Mind if I join you?" I asked and didn't wait for an answer.

I pulled myself out of the window and sat next to him. The sky was turning pink and orange as the afternoon set in, sprinkled with thousands of green fireflies.

"How are you holding up?"

He shrugged. A man of few words, as usual.

"Listen, you should stop beating yourself up over those fire-flies. You couldn't have known. I probably would've done the same if I saw them and didn't know what they were," I said.

Field let out a sigh and looked at me with a pained expression.

"I put everyone at risk, Phoenix, including you."

"Will you snap out of it, already? It wasn't your fault."

He didn't say anything for a while, as we watched the Destroyers together.

"We've got our hands full now," I said. "We should find weaknesses in these monsters. They must have some soft spots."

"I heard Sverik say that fire kills them, as does decapitation," Field muttered.

"Have you picked up any patterns so far in how they operate?"

He pointed at Goren down below, who was slumped against a tree, sharpening his sword with a black rock.

"He's the leader. That I can tell you for sure. The others don't do anything without his consent. They all look at him when they talk to each other. I think they fear him."

"Given the size of the guy, I can't really blame them," I said.

I instantly thought of everything we stood to lose if Vita's vision came true. My sister, my friends, the Daughter—they all represented pain points that throbbed at the thought of Destroyers getting past the protective shield.

"One of Vita's visions showed Destroyers getting inside the house," I told him.

Field's gaze darkened as he nodded slowly.

"I heard Vita say it. How?" he managed to ask.

"I have no idea. She couldn't see more than the actual invasion," I replied. "But I know one thing for sure, Field. We *can't* let these monsters win. We've got to win— not just for Eritopia, but for The Shade and for GASP."

A moment passed before I spoke again, since I wasn't done with the gloom and doom just yet.

"Vita saw Jovi die, as well, in the battle against Azazel," I said, my voice barely audible.

Field turned his head, staring at me in disbelief.

"What did you just say?"

"Jovi will die, according to Vita's visions. I guess we have our work cut out for us..."

"There's no way I'm letting anyone die. Not on my watch they won't," he shook his head vehemently.

"I completely agree. We are fighting this all the way through, man."

Given the stern look on his face, I knew he'd found the determination he needed to move ahead. The mention of our home and family was more than enough to snap him back into action.

"We have to make our parents proud and protect the women we're so mindlessly in love with," I added with a smirk.

I was telling the truth, though. I was in love with the Daughter. There was no doubt left in my mind. As for Field, it wasn't difficult to see he was head over his heels whenever he was near Aida. The simple mention of her made him beam like a lighthouse.

He smiled, watching one Destroyer trying his luck with a large hammer against the shield. The creature failed miserably, the blow throwing him back a few feet as golden sparks shot out.

"I think it's fair to remind you that the women we're in love with can pretty much take care of themselves without our assistance," he replied, his tone playful.

I could feel the Field I knew rising back to the surface, and I knew I had the right guy at my side to fight whatever came at us, as always.

"I can only imagine what would happen if someone tried to mess with the Daughter." I chuckled.

She'd come a long way since her brief encounter with that shape-shifter. The trauma had strengthened her in ways I hadn't thought possible but welcomed nonetheless. She was sure of her words, she communicated more, and she asked more questions. With each step she took she came closer to the knowledge and godlike power surging inside of her.

"A Daughter can kill you with a single touch." Field grinned.

"You might want to be careful, Phoenix. Do not forget her birthday. That's all I can say."

I snorted in response. "You deal with yours, and I'll deal with mine, Field, because I'll bet you anything that Aida's wrath could be just as deadly. Remember that time I stole her clothes while she showered after practice, like two years ago?" I grinned as I recalled the race over the training grounds with a fired-up, towel-clad Aida on my trail.

"Yeah, I think you broke the speed record then."

I laughed. "Those were good times."

Field's tone suddenly went serious. "More good times will come once we get rid of these overgrown snakes."

Our moment of levity was over. I took a deep breath and got a better look at two Destroyers riding their flying horses overhead. I still couldn't fathom how they would get past the shield.

"If they do get in," Field said, "we'll need one of us to draw them out. Distract them."

I glanced at him and noticed a shadow swiftly passing over his face. "What do you mean?" I asked.

"I'll fly out and draw them out. I'm the only one capable of giving them a good run for their money, given my wings," he replied. "Should worse come to worst, I'll take one for the team."

"Field—"

"Listen to me, Phoenix. It's settled. Nothing more to talk about. Just promise me you'll look after Aida if I don't make it. That's all. Just take care of her."

I didn't want to consider one of my best friends dying. That wasn't on the menu. It wasn't part of the plan, and I would never allow him to do something so foolish. But Field could be stubborn as hell, and once he set his mind on something, it was nearly impossible to convince him otherwise.

But that was the old Field, I thought. The Field who hadn't discovered Aida yet. I knew something had changed inside of him from the moment they got closer, so I decided to exploit that and persuade him to think twice and not throw himself into death's arms so easily. He had noble ambitions, but there had to be a better way.

"Hate to break it to you, my friend, but Aida will never let you perish like that." I smirked. "She will rip you out of the leathery claws of death herself and beat you to a pulp, if she has to. She won't let you die."

Field gave me a sad smile, his turquoise eyes glimmering with what might have been tears. I couldn't be sure, as he looked away for a moment.

He turned his gaze on me again. The glimmer was gone. I had a feeling I'd managed to pluck a more sensitive chord in him, so I decided to double down, just to be sure he got my point.

"She'd never forgive you, Field. Don't mess with Aida, man. You're stuck with her." I grinned.

He finally mirrored my expression and nodded. I felt relieved I'd won that little battle.

7

VITA

As everyone was focused on Draven and Serena's impending excursion, I decided to tell Bijarki the whole vision of the Destroyers invading the building. I'd deliberately left important details out—important to me and him, but not to the group. I needed to tell *him* the whole story.

He was talking to Sverik on one side of the table, while Draven, Serena, and Hansa conferred on the other side. I walked up to him, feeling my palms sweat.

How am I going to tell him?

"Can we talk for a moment?" I asked.

He looked up at me, then at Sverik, who nodded and moved to a seat closer to Draven to join their conversation. Bijarki waited for me to speak.

"Not here," I mumbled and walked out.

I looked over my shoulder and saw him stand up and follow me. We went upstairs, to the study room where we'd first kissed. The memory instantly invaded me with warmth as I remembered the way he had responded to my kiss.

I leaned against the writing desk.

He closed the door behind him. His silvery eyes glimmered, as if he was thinking about the same moment, but his expression was still.

It took me a minute to gather the courage to tell him the whole account of my vision, during which time he waited patiently, his body inches from mine. I could feel his incubus nature unravel slowly. A pleasant lightheadedness took over. I shuddered, trying to keep a clear head.

He noticed my reaction and instantly brought himself under control.

"I didn't tell them everything about my vision," I started. "The one with Destroyers invading the mansion. I left out some details."

"What is it you left out, then?"

He wasn't making it any easier, looking at me the way he did with desire oozing from his every pore even with his incubus nature turned off. I had to figure out a way to tell him that we'd end up in bed together and that I would, for one brief moment in my existence, feel like the happiest creature in the world with his body so close to mine. I'd never experienced that kind of intimacy before, and despite the novels I'd read growing up, I still had a hard time finding the right words to describe it.

"I wasn't alone in the room when they came for me," I mumbled. "I was with you."

Our eyes met, and I could see his gaze soften as he lowered his head. The silver pools surrounding his pupils seemed to ripple outward, as he pictured the scene for himself.

"What was I doing in your room in the middle of the night?"

A playful smile passed over his lips, a mere flicker of intentional humor meant to remove some of the stress. I'd seen the way he'd looked at me when I spoke of Destroyers taking me. I could tell he'd been floored by the thought of losing me to Azazel's monsters. I couldn't blame him for attempting to make light of the situation.

Nevertheless, it didn't stop my cheeks from catching fire as I tried to find the appropriate words to describe our bare bodies together, tucked away beneath the sheets while the moonlight poured through the windows and made his skin shimmer even more beautifully.

I took a deep breath and let it out slowly, as if delaying the inevitable.

"We were in bed together. No clothes. I... I think we... You know..."

I sounded more coherent than I'd expected, given my natural shyness. It wasn't something I was used to talking about, not even with Serena and Aida. And I told them everything.

Bijarki smiled gently, taking a step forward and closing the distance between us. Our bodies touched. His firm and imposing frame pressed against mine. I felt so tiny and helpless.

He bent forward and caught my mouth in a soft, sweet kiss. I welcomed him as his arms wrapped around me, and he paused to look at me.

"I find your blushing endearing," he whispered and kissed me again, briefly. "And sweet."

"I... I'm..."

I tried to speak, but I felt tears stinging my eyes as I gently pushed him away, putting a foot between us. My body trembled as I tried to keep it together.

"I watched them attack us... Attack you... You were down, Bijarki, and I... I can't... I'm terrified. Please understand. I am terrified of anything happening to you."

I sobbed, no longer able to control myself. The pain caused by the mere thought of watching him get hurt tore into me worse than anything else I'd experienced so far in this world.

He let out a breath and took me in his arms again, this time unyielding when I tried to push him away. I was too weak to fight it anymore, anyway. I leaned my head against his broad chest and cried some more, letting it all out as he held me tightly.

He ran his fingers through my hair and cupped my cheek, lifting my head so he could look into my eyes. His expression was soft. His skin glowed with intense emotions that I yearned to believe involved the same kind of love that had started to bloom inside of me.

"Don't cry, Vita," he said quietly, dropping a kiss on the tip of my nose. "I promise you, I swear to you, in fact, that I will do everything in my power to stop that vision from coming true. Do you hear me?"

I nodded, swallowing back another wave of tears as his words filled me with something so powerful that it made every muscle in my body shudder.

"But I—"

"Nothing more to say, darling." He stopped my feeble protest, as if knowing what I was going to say. "Nothing. Don't think for a second I'll be able to stay away from you, even if that future you saw could come true. There's no way I'm keeping my distance now, not when I know that the very future that sees us die is the same that brings us together in ways I've been dreaming about since I first laid eyes on you."

Bijarki let out a deep breath and pulled me even closer, tightening his embrace. I was so soft in his arms, so easy to break, yet so complete and liberated, on the very edge of bliss. Darkness loomed around us, but Bijarki was the light I followed, the beacon that kept me on track and beckoned me to stand up and fight.

"Vita," he whispered in my ear. "I cannot wait to feel you, all of you. We'll just have to make sure there aren't any nasty Destroyers to ruin the moment. That's all."

I couldn't stop a chuckle from escaping the back of my throat. He made it sound so easy.

The way he looked at me had a strange way of assuring me that he would certainly do everything he could to stop that horrible future from happening. It may not have meant much to anyone else, but his words of promise were all I had to go on.

And given the circumstances, I was happy to take that over the possibility of my vision coming true.

8

SERENA

We gathered in the banquet hall once more about two hours later. The Daughter had managed to translate several useful spells, while Phoenix and Anjani helped gather the ingredients needed for each formula.

The Daughter handed us the scrolls, which I stuffed in my satchel, along with half of the herbs, powder, and various other paraphernalia required. Draven filled his bag with whatever didn't fit in mine.

"Along with the fire protection and invisibility spells, you've got a light in the dark formula and several poison healing concoctions, including one that will help counteract Destroyer venom," the Daughter said.

"Light in the dark?" I asked.

"It's what it's called in the witches' book. It's a spell cast on a regular object for it to emit light, a simple verbal incantation I thought might come in handy. That's all I could gather at such short notice. There are other spells in there, but they take longer to prepare, and some of the ingredients can only be found in specific places, from what Anjani has told me. None are close enough for us to reach in time."

I nodded as I pulled the string on my new satchel, one of the three that Draven had brought down from the attic, with a thick textile membrane lining to help keep it waterproof. I mounted it on my back, tying makeshift bands over my shoulders and around my waist to keep it tight and fixed. Given that we didn't know where the passage stone would take us, I had to make sure we had maximum mobility, so I'd sewn additional straps to each of our travel bags.

Draven, Hansa, Sverik, and I said our goodbyes. Phoenix came up to me and took me in a heavy bear hug, making me giggle as he lifted me off the ground. He smiled, but I could tell he was worried from the way his emotions flared at me. We'd been around each other for so long that our sentry powers were attuned to each other's feelings. We didn't need to reach out to understand what the other was experiencing. We just knew.

Since I'd bonded so deeply with Draven, as had Phoenix with the Daughter, we were constantly well "fed" with the powerful energy that they gave off. I could sense the Daughter's life force coursing through my brother, and I was pretty sure he could sense Draven's in me. As sentries, we'd found our "endless supply" of strength.

"You know I'm expecting you back in one piece, as usual,

right?" he quipped, cupping my face and dropping a kiss on my forehead.

His warmth enveloped me, and I welcomed it like a protective layer that would help me against whatever waited beyond the stone.

"I'm well aware, big brother," I said, forcing a confident smile.

I wasn't sure it was the case, though. We didn't know what we were walking into, but I couldn't bring myself to share that thought with Phoenix. I needed him strong, hopeful, and focused to help the others.

"Phoenix, Aida, Vita," Draven addressed the Oracles while tying up his satchel straps. "I need you to keep digging through your visions while we're away. Focus on anything that could help us going forward, particularly any weaknesses in Azazel's den. Write everything down, and have someone record the runes that appear during each session."

My brother and two best friends nodded solemnly. They followed us outside, along with Jovi, Anjani, the Daughter, and Field. The two Lamias stayed behind, not feeling too chatty after our biting back-and-forth from earlier. To be honest, I wasn't too keen on seeing them either. If I was to die, I didn't want their smug and self-satisfied smirks to be the last thing I saw.

Draven was the first to go down the stairs into the grotto. I went in second, followed by Hansa and Sverik. The others waved goodbye as we descended.

Once we reached the massive black passage stone, Draven looked at me, then at Hansa and Sverik.

"Are you all ready?" he asked.

"Ready as we'll ever be." I gave him a weak smile.

My heart shrank inside my chest as I inadvertently obsessed over all possible scenarios of our destination. I took a deep breath, letting my anxiety out in controlled slow-motion.

"I'm nowhere near as prepared as I should be, but I've been through worse. I mean, what's the worst that could happen, right?" Sverik chuckled nervously behind me.

"We could die," Hansa's reply was blunt and merciless.

I stifled a grin as I looked over my shoulder and saw the incubus's expression fade into something akin to despair. Then I remembered something from our first alternative travel experience back at the Red Tribe.

"Hansa drew your blood the first time we used the passage stone in her tent," I said to Draven. "Doesn't it need blood?"

"It needs the blood of someone who's seen the other stone," he replied, his gaze fixed on the smooth obsidian surface. "In this case, the only stone we've seen is the one most likely now in Azazel's private chamber. And that is the last place we want to visit today," He looked at Sverik. "However, you are right. It does need blood. Sverik, have you ever seen a passage stone before?"

"Not that I can remember, no. We prefer horses." He smirked.

"Good. Give me your hand."

"Why?"

"Stop asking stupid questions, and give the Druid your hand," Hansa snapped and gave him a nudge.

Sverik grumbled and extended his right hand as Draven took out a small pocket knife and nicked the palm. The incubus cursed under his breath as silver blood bloomed from the cut.

"Put your hand on the stone," Draven instructed him. "Because you've never seen one before, your lack of knowledge will take us to a random stone. If you had seen one before, it would most likely take us to that specific stone, because it's attuned to your memory."

We all knew the drill. I took Sverik's hand, and Draven took mine and Hansa's. The path, despite being short, was bound to be pitch black. We couldn't risk losing each other.

The obsidian surface began its familiar ripple outward in thin, vibrant rings.

The incubus walked through it first. I took a deep breath and followed, feeling the cold embrace of the stone and Draven's firm grip on my hand.

9

SERENA

The darkness cleared like mist as I walked into the warm sunlight waiting on the other side of the passage stone. My relief was short-lived, as I saw Sverik right in front of me, gasping before he disappeared from my line of sight.

I took another step to see where he had vanished, then felt the solid ground disappear from under my feet. I fell from a great height. A turquoise blue mass of water waited beneath. My instincts kicked in, and I braced myself for the impact, realizing what had happened.

I hit the water hard, wishing I'd practiced my barrier skills more so I could break my fall. The air whooshed from my lungs. I sank like lead. I opened my eyes and saw Sverik swimming back to the surface and strange movement farther away in the water. The bottom was clean and sandy. I made my way back up, ignoring the pain in my bones, particularly on my right side.

Two more bodies joined us in the water. Draven and Hansa had also fallen in.

My head pushed through the surface, and I took a deep breath, taking in the stunning view around us. The obsidian stone was perched on a sharp black cliff, and we'd fallen into what looked like a blue lagoon. Thick purple and yellow trees lined the water, and white sand formed a thin strip of beach all around. The sky above us was a watercolor array of oranges and pinks, riddled with puffs of white clouds.

"Are you okay?" Draven made it to the surface and swam toward me.

"Yeah, still here!" I replied, then looked at Hansa and Sverik.

We'd made it. In one piece, too. Despite the initial shock of the fall, I felt relief once again washing over me. I was thankful that I would live to fight another day. We smiled at each other, most likely thinking the same thing.

I caught shadows out of the corner of my eye, moving swiftly beneath the water.

"Good to see we made it," Sverik exclaimed.

"Wait," I managed to say. "There's something—"

Before I could finish, Draven disappeared underwater. Sverik followed three seconds later. I screamed while Hansa cursed, and the next thing I knew, slippery fingers were wrapping around my ankles. I was suddenly submerged. I struggled to make my way back up to the surface.

My survival instinct went into overdrive quickly. I pushed out a mental barrier at whatever was attacking us, and it released me. I opened my eyes in the clear water and was stunned.

Dozens of creatures swam around us, poking, prodding, and pulling. I stilled, recognizing the half-humanoid, half-fish forms. These were some type of merfolk, from what I could tell, making our predicament far more dangerous than I'd initially thought. But they looked so very different from the merfolk I was used to. They didn't appear to be vicious animals with fangs and a horrifying appetite for human flesh. These all had long hair in light shades of blond and long colorful tails, varying from one creature to another. Their features were beautiful, with large eyes and bright smiles. They didn't seem vicious at all, but evasive and, for lack of a better word, playful.

I watched Draven, Sverik, and Hansa as they struggled against the creatures' antics. Then another one of them came at me, swimming faster than I could react.

It pushed me, then swam away. It was a male, with a long tail in bright shades of orange and white, resembling that of a Koi fish. He had a large translucent fin running the length of his spine and a pleasing frame. There were muscles beneath his smooth skin, but they were not big enough to disrupt the overall fluidity of his body. His features were surprising. I was looking at a young man, probably in his early twenties, with pale blue eyes and long pale blonde hair.

He came at me again, but this time I was ready as I focused on him and reached out to control his mind. I felt myself touching his mind, but nothing happened. He still swam to me and smiled with pearly white teeth. No fangs. He reached out with what appeared to be perfectly normal hands, pushed me again, and swam away.

The others continued to annoy Draven, Sverik, and Hansa, but less so than before. We all managed to swim back to the surface, gasping for air with the creatures bumping into us underwater.

"Don't hurt them!" I spluttered to the others. "I don't think they want to harm us!"

I'd barely spoken the words before I got pulled back under, and I heard Draven's muffled voice shouting after me from above. The young merman who had pushed me earlier was the same one gripping my hand and keeping me submerged. I tried to pull back, but he tightened his grip and smiled again, a glimmer in his eyes challenging me to fight back.

Two can play that game. I gave him a grin before I pushed out a barrier. It took him by surprise, knocking him back a few feet. I returned to the surface. The others struggled against their own merfolk, who tugged at and pulled them under the surface.

"These are merfolk," I managed to say to Draven once he made it back up. "But they don't look or behave like the ones I've seen."

"That's because they're not merfolk," Draven replied dryly, his tone decidedly annoyed by now.

He muttered something under his breath, closed his eyes, and a bright light expanded from his body beneath the water.

The creatures stilled and one by one bobbed up to the surface, leaving Sverik and Hansa alone as well.

The young male I'd tackled popped out right in front of me, his blue eyes scanning me inquisitively. I looked around at the myriad of azure eyes now watching us. I was able to get a better look at them now that they were above water. Their skin was pale. The males were adorned with the same large, semi-transparent back fin, while the females had smaller, more delicate ones protruding from their wrists. They all wore a mixture of shells and gemstones around their necks and no other garments.

"Greetings," the young male said to me, as serene as a summer morning.

"They're Tritones," Draven finally replied.

It took me a second to register the information. I couldn't take my eyes off the creature in front of me. He cocked his head and smiled once more.

"Tritones," I repeated. The name reminded me of ancient Greek legends and Triton, King of the Seas. I wondered if there was a connection.

"Tritones," the young one mimicked me.

I smiled back at him uncertainly, finding myself fascinated but still unnerved by his species. My heart continued to rattle beneath my ribs. Were we really safe, or were these just a beautiful kind of merfolk who happened to like playing with their food?

10

AIDA

Soon after Serena and Draven went through the passage stone, Field and I escaped to the roof. He flew, and I held on. I needed to talk with him and make sure he was okay. I knew him well enough to understand that the whole green firefly incident affected him more than he let on and that he could use some company.

We sat at the very edge, watching Destroyers and fireflies roaming around, as if watching a movie at the IMAX. Some time passed before either of us spoke. But I was comfortable with that. We didn't always need words to fill the space. Being close to each other was more than enough.

"I've been thinking," he said slowly, "about ways to get out of here, in case everything goes south, or in case we simply have to leave."

"Vita's vision, right?" I figured it was one of the reasons why he'd been thinking of possible ways out.

He nodded. "We have to think of every possible option, considering what's lurking outside and the clear possibility that they could get in somehow."

"There's the passage stone," I mused.

"We can simply walk out, as well."

"With Destroyers waiting outside, eager to tear us apart?"

"We need to start considering alternatives, a way to perhaps distract them and get us a clear path out of here," he replied, looking out.

I leaned against him and rested my head on his shoulder. I could feel the tension in his muscles dissipate.

"The plants for the invisibility spell are running low," I said. "And it will take months before we can grow more ingredients in the greenhouse."

"You know, Azazel's taken a lot of interest in this shield, given the number of Destroyers and fireflies he's stationed here. Sooner or later, he might find a way in. I don't think he'll give up so easily."

He had a point. Azazel was not one to quit until he got what he wanted. And we didn't know the Daughters well enough to have a guarantee that they'd be able to permanently keep him out.

"What if we try to reach out to the Daughters?" I asked.

Field shrugged. "Worth a shot, but how can we do that without the Druid?"

"Maybe Anjani knows more about that prayer dust? I mean, the succubi did it and got an answer." I thought out loud, remembering my vision.

I looked out, watching Goren as he barked more orders at his Destroyers. I used my heightened wolf senses to get a better look and sniff out any of the chemicals that they were letting off. I could sense fear and a permanent feeling of displeasure, like they were miserable in their skins. They didn't make eye contact with Goren but nodded every time he said something.

It reminded me of the conversation I'd overheard between Goren and Patrik about Azazel's influence and how it poisoned the bodies and souls to the point where they had no other choice but obey him. The scent of frustration coming off them must be the result of their struggle with their situation.

"No matter what happens, Aida," Field said, his voice low, "I won't let anything happen to you."

I gazed up at him, and something flickered in his turquoise eyes, a flash of sorts that ignited something in my soul.

"I know you won't," I whispered.

He sighed. "It's just that this whole mess with the fireflies, I know it's stupid but it still bugs me." He allowed himself a tiny, albeit pained, smile. "Pun not intended. I wanted to do something nice, show you something cool. I'm aware that there was no way I could've known what they were, but I can't help but feel like such a dunce."

I couldn't bear to see him like this. He was still chastising himself over those stupid green bugs, and I just wanted to take those negative emotions and throw them as far away from him as possible.

"Let's not dwell on the past," I said. "Everything that happened, happened, Field. Let's focus on what's ahead. As twisted as it may sound, with all the dangers lurking around us, I actually like where this is going." I pointed at him and me.

Then I took a deep breath, my mind wandering back to my brother.

"I just can't shake this whole Jovi dying thing off," I said. "I can't accept it. I don't know what I'd do without him, he's like a part of me. I keep trying to think of ways to stop that vision from coming true."

"Aida, you have my word that no matter what happens, I will make sure that Jovi stays alive and irritating like he is. There's no way anyone in our Shade family is dying on my watch. Not even the loud-mouth wolf-boy." Field smiled and wrapped his arm around me, pulling me closer to him. I relaxed against him, my hand resting on his chest. I could feel his heart beneath my palm, beating faster. His lips pressed against my forehead, soft and hot, searing through my core.

"I will look after you, Aida. I'll keep you safe, and we'll all make it back to The Shade in one piece," he whispered.

I closed my eyes for a moment, imagining that scenario— me and him walking among the redwoods, our parents waiting for us on the forest path with arms wide open, smiling and happy. The mere idea stretched my lips into a smile.

I raised my eyes to meet his gaze and touched his face,

letting my fingers slide gently down the ridge of his cheek. My heart was full of wonderful things, each fueled by the way he looked at me, the sound of his voice, the feel of his lips on mine, and the way we were together—better, stronger, and more complete.

"I'll do the same for you, Field. I promise," I replied. "We've only just found each other, Hawk. There's no way I'm losing you."

His gaze softened, and another faint smile passed over his face. He kissed me, and our souls fused once more.

11

VITA

As the sun set in deep shades of pink and red, I went outside. I brought a candle with me, playing with its flame as I walked around the garden. Watching the monsters hissing and prowling outside made me want to reinforce my own ability to protect myself against potential attacks, especially after what the future had shown me.

I'd developed enough of a skill to burn a few of them down if I wanted to and, for a minute, I was tempted, too. But Draven had already advised against it. Nobody was supposed to know we were in here. So, we couldn't give ourselves or our abilities away. It would've just brought more of them in, and increased Azazel's interest in what lay within the shield.

My heart wavered every time my mind wandered toward Bijarki. I couldn't help but worry—about him, about me, about all of us. My fingers trembled above the flame causing it to flicker and grow. I beckoned it to follow my lead and swirled it up in a spiral, moving my hand upward and bringing along tendrils of flame.

An uncontrollable sadness descended on me. The fire dimmed and then died out. I was having a hard time focusing. I took a deep breath and looked up.

Bijarki sat at the base of a magnolia tree, his back leaning against the trunk. He gazed out, watching the Destroyers as they set up camp beyond the shield. Something glistened in his hand. His elbow rested on his knee—it looked like a delicate silver chain with a pendant dangling at the end.

I took a step forward, and a twig broke under my foot.

The sound made Bijarki turn his head. His gaze found mine. His eyes widened, and his skin suddenly glowed as he clutched the pendant and shoved it in his pocket. He then gave me a weak smile and patted the grass next to him.

I smiled back and sat down, leaning gently against him. He gestured to the candle in my hands and looked at me inquisitively. I wanted to ask Bijarki about the pendant. I opened my mouth, but he was swift in steering the conversation away.

"Practicing?" he asked.

I nodded. "I figured it wouldn't hurt to get a better grip on fire."

"As you should. According to the Dearghs, fire burns everything, even snakes."

We both watched the Destroyers for a while. I was learning to adjust to the hollow feeling in the pit of my stomach that persisted whenever I got close to the monsters waiting outside. They weren't going anywhere any time soon. I had to get used to them being around. I couldn't allow their presence to cloud my judgment or diminish my capacity to defend myself or the ones I loved.

"Goren seems to be the only leader around here. They only listen to him," Bijarki said, his gaze fixed on the bulky Destroyer.

The snake sat in front of a campfire, grinning to himself as he warmed up. It was still summer outside with dry, hot air persisting even in the late hours of the afternoon, but given his serpent nature, I assumed he appreciated the additional heat like Draven.

"From what Aida told us, they're not happy to be what they are. At least some of them aren't happy," I replied.

"You can tell from the way they behave, particularly around Goren. They avoid eye contact, and they jump every time he raises his voice."

"I wonder how they must have felt when they conceded to Azazel in the first place."

"They probably thought they were doing the right thing, living to fight another day." Bijarki sighed. "By the time Azazel's magic worked them over, it was too late for them to resist. Their will succumbed, and they found themselves stuck as his snake-tailed puppets."

I rested my head on his shoulder, seeking the warmth that

his body emanated. I needed the comfort of his presence. With everything going on, it felt so good to have him near me.

"What alliances can be made against him?" I asked. "What else can we do to defeat him?"

"Everything we're doing right now is building up to one final battle," he replied. "Every pawn, every move, it all leads us across the board, closer to the king, until we all get close enough to cut the snake's head off and rid this world of his poison. Alliances are not easy to come by these days. Most of Azazel's enemies have been wiped out or reduced to a handful of rogue settlements scattered across the planets."

"What about other Druids?" I asked. "I mean, I know Draven said they were all turned or killed, but do we know that for sure, beyond a shadow of doubt?"

Bijarki shook his head.

"We don't. But we figured we would have seen one or heard of one by now. Marchosi was the last standing Druid I knew of, and he's obviously gone. Almus's planet was decimated when Azazel invaded it. Scores upon scores of young Druids, some with just a few years in this world, were slaughtered in the process. And yet, there is no absolute certainty that there aren't any left somewhere, perhaps hiding as we speak."

It then occurred to me to ask Aida and Phoenix to focus on that during our next visions. I couldn't think of much I could probe with the future, but the past and present would surely yield some answers about other Druids. And since Draven had taught us how to focus on specific periods and subjects as

Oracles, I figured it would be another great opportunity to practice. After all, it had worked surprisingly well during the last round.

Phoenix showed up on the lawn to our left, looking around nervously, his eyes wide and gaze darting left and right. His breath was ragged. He'd been running.

"Phoenix," I called out, capturing his attention. "Are you okay?"

He shook his head. "I can't find the Daughter," he said. "She was in the banquet hall with me, going over the swamp witches' spells. I looked away for a minute, and she was gone, and now I can't find her!"

Bijarki and I sprang to our feet and scanned our surroundings. It took us a few minutes to find her. Phoenix used his True Sight on the eastern edge of the property, but Bijarki was the first to point in her direction on the opposite side. I recognized her beautiful reddish pink hair flowing down her back.

I had to squint to get a better look.

My breath hitched. She was standing in front of Goren.

12

PHOENIX

My heart stopped. My blood froze.

The Daughter was about fifty yards from us on the western edge of the property, barely inches from Goren.

"Get away from him!" I shouted and darted toward her.

Vita and Bijarki ran after me. I reached her in seconds, only to realize that she hadn't left the protective shield and that Goren wasn't aware of her presence there. Or ours, for that matter.

I opened my mouth to ask what the hell she was thinking, but I stopped myself at the sight of her violet eyes glowing like incandescent lightbulbs. She stared at the massive Destroyer. Her breathing was even, and she was calm. Her gaze was absent yet fixed on Goren, who was busy ordering his Destroyers around, occasionally reaching a hand out to the fire behind him. He looked around, his eyes squinting, probably wondering what was beyond the invisible shield.

"Don't let this whole area out of your sights!" he barked. "Someone's in there. I know it. I just can't see the little birdies. But sooner or later, they'll have to come out."

"What are you doing?" Vita asked the Daughter.

There was no response. The Daughter was still and quiet, eyes beaming as she watched the Destroyer.

"His name is Goren, son of Kalispera and Osteus, both Druids of the Ninth Kingdom," she said, her voice sounding like a million people overlapped, speaking as one.

It sent chills down my spine.

"Kalispera and Osteus never acquired all their rings. Kalispera only got fifty, and Osteus got sixty-seven, so they were considered of lower rank, barely of administrative capabilities in the Ninth Kingdom," the Daughter continued. "Goren happened by mistake and was the reason they were married in the first place. For many years, they both blamed his birth for their failure to ascend as Druids. Goren grew up with that weight on his shoulders, constantly feeling inadequate. Osteus often beat him as a child, taking out his frustrations on him.

"By the time Goren made it into his eighteenth year, it was his turn to beat Osteus. But he didn't stop at a few payback punches. Goren beat his father into the grave and enrolled in the Druid Academy, never seeing his grieving mother again. He became an aggressor, a fighter, a violent creature with hatred buried deep beneath his muscles."

We all looked at Goren and listened as the Daughter told us his entire life's story in astonishing detail, from his first crush to his last Druid ring before he became a Destroyer willingly. And it all sort of made sense. I could see the frustration in his yellow eyes, the undertones of guilt and anger that had been his companions for centuries.

"Goren never got his hundredth ring, although he'd often seen himself as the next ruler of the Ninth Kingdom. In fact, Goren never made it past his thirty-seventh ring when Azazel invaded his planet and made him an offer he found he didn't want to refuse. Goren accepted Azazel's offer. He was given an army of treacherous incubi and a legion of Destroyers to obey his every command. In return, he allowed Azazel's dark poison to eat away at him, until he lost his Druid form and magic and became what he is today, the slithering sum of all his poor choices, each fueled by his desire to show his dead father that his birth had not been in vain."

Vita, Bijarki, and I looked at each other in awe, listening as the Daughter then told us Goren's future—also in mind-blowing detail.

"Goren will not live for much longer," she said in her million voices. "His head will roll down the black marble stairs of Luceria. His body will burn, and a succubus will laugh as the flames consume him and remove every trace of him in this world. He will die the same way he has lived—cruel, vindictive, and bloody."

"What's Luceria?" I asked, my voice barely a whisper.

"It's Azazel's castle on this planet," Bijarki replied. "It once belonged to Genevieve, Draven's mother. It was her royal residence."

"The one made of black marble and stone," Vita gasped.

"Yes."

"It's where all roads end," said the Daughter. Her eyes rolled back, and she passed out.

I caught her before she hit the ground. I took her in my arms and headed toward the mansion, surprised that I myself hadn't passed out with her.

Vita tried to follow, but Bijarki stopped her.

"She needs rest," the incubus said.

I glanced at him over my shoulder and nodded, then looked at the Daughter, fragile and unconscious in my arms. Whatever the heck that had been, it had taken its toll on her. My heart thudded in my chest as I flew into the house and up the stairs to my room.

I laid her on the bed, brushing locks of her reddish pink hair away from her pale beautiful face. Her eyes were closed, her lips parted. I listened to her breathing as I sat next to her.

With a single glance, she'd been able to look at a creature like Goren and tell his entire story, from conception to death, without ever having seen, spoken to, or even heard of him before. The concept of omniscience sprang to life in the back of my head, and I wondered whether she'd be able to do the same with me, my sister, and my friends.

Would she be able to tell our stories the same way, from

beginning to end, as if we were just another few pages in a giant book of Eritopia? We weren't born here, so maybe she wouldn't be able to. Though something told me that our Oracle abilities tied us to this place.

As I looked down at the Daughter and watched her sleep, I wondered how long my story would last.

13

JOVI

We took turns patrolling the edge of the shield to further analyze and understand how the Destroyers operated. We needed to identify their weak spots and hope there were lots of them.

Anjani and I took the first shift as the sky turned indigo and glinted with stars. We walked along the shield for a while, watching Destroyers gather in clusters of five and six in front of small fires. Some returned with fresh kills from the woods, sharing the raw meat.

My gag reflex threatened me as I watched them swallow creatures whole, their jaws opening unnaturally wide, like the half-serpents they were.

"That is just...disgusting," I managed.

"You thought the fires were for cooking?" Anjani's question was rhetorical, her eyebrow raised at me.

"Seriously? They warm up to it but can't figure out a way to use it to cook their food?" I couldn't fathom eating raw meat. If I'd been a full wolf, I probably would've stomached the concept better, but the mere thought turned me inside out.

"Destroyers are very primitive. They eat the animals whole and raw. They swallow, digest, then regurgitate the bones and other parts that cannot make it through their digestive tract," Anjani explained.

It took me a while before the information really hit me.

"Oh," I scoffed. "And is Draven the same? He hunts critters, gobbles them up, and then spits their bones out later?"

She shrugged. We slowed our pace as we passed by a patch of thick woods submerged in darkness.

"Pretty much, yes. Although I know he's very private about it, from what Bijarki told me. I haven't seen him feed since I've been here," she said.

"Yeah, me neither. I didn't need this level of detail, I shouldn't have asked... I just can't look at him the same way anymore."

"He's still Draven."

"Yeah, but jeez. Serena will have to watch out for her parents' pet lynx if the guy ever visits The Shade."

Anjani laughed lightly, and I enjoyed every second of her crystalline voice, but our moment was short-lived.

A rustle in the leaves beyond the shield drew our attention. We both stilled, watching the obscure forest in front of us. A branch broke. I focused my attention on the source of the noise and saw several shadows moving toward us.

I heard Anjani gasp. I recognized the succubi from her tribe. There were twelve of them, two barely reaching their teenage years, poking their heads out through the dense foliage. They looked around, then ahead, frowning.

"What do we do?" one of them whispered.

"The area ahead is too open. They'll kill us before we reach the other side," another whispered back.

"By the Daughters," Anjani mumbled. "They're the survivors Aida mentioned! We need to get them in here!"

I looked to our right, then our left and froze at the sight of three Destroyers approaching. A couple more yards, and they would find the succubi hiding in the bushes in front of us.

"We have to do something, Jovi," Anjani's tone gained urgency.

She stilled for a moment, then darted beyond the shield.

"Anjani, wait!" I croaked, but it was too late.

She'd gone past the protective spell and could no longer see or hear me. She shot through the small clearing several yards away, unseen by her sisters. She passed the Destroyers and smacked one over the face before she vanished between the trees.

The creatures were befuddled for a second. They hissed and slithered after her, drawing their spears. They went into the dark woods, and I could no longer see them.

My heart raced. I cursed under my breath. Anjani had done

a very reckless thing, but I couldn't blame her. She was diverting the Destroyers' attention from her sisters, which meant I had to step in.

From what I understood, the ancient wards in charge of this protective shield registered all those who entered, allowing them to return whenever they wished. The Druid had once said that he had control over who could pass through the shield and that anyone he'd allowed in could bring someone else with them, provided there was some form of physical contact.

The coast was clear, and I took a step forward through the shield, making myself partially visible to the succubi. They all stared at me, eyes bulging, probably wondering how they could only see part of me.

"Come here," I whispered, offering them my hand. "It's a magic shield. You can't see anything beyond it!"

One of them came out of the bush and cocked her head, frowning at me.

"You're Anjani's mate," she whispered. "Where is she?"

"On her way back, and we have no time for this! Take my hand, then have your sisters hold hands with you, so I can bring you all in. It's the only way this will work."

I found her frown irritating, as if I wasn't good enough for her sister, or something equally untrue. But my ego could wait. She was prompt in her response and took my hand, beckoning the others to hold on to her. The others nodded and quietly stepped out.

She looked over her shoulder to make sure they were all in contact, then shifted her focus back on me.

"We're ready," she muttered.

I pulled her in, and the others followed. I couldn't help but grin when I saw it had worked. I'd managed to bring the succubi in to safety.

They all looked around, marveling at the mansion, the lush garden, the Destroyers, and the green fireflies' inability to get past the shield.

"This is incredible," one of them said.

They talked among each other as I waited on the edge of the shield. My eyes searched for Anjani. She was out there some-where, running away from three extremely pissed off Destroy-ers. My heart pounded as I listened for any sound that could tell me whether she was coming back.

A minute passed. One of the succubi approached my side as she gazed beyond the shield.

"Where's Anjani, wolf-boy?"

"She ran out to create a diversion for you all to get in here safely. She should be back any second now," I murmured.

"You let her out?" her tone was sharp and accusative.

"Since when did you think I could control a succubus like her?"

"Fair enough," she conceded.

Anjani would've ignored me completely even if I'd advised against it before she ran off. Not to mention she would've smacked me ten ways to Sunday if I'd forbidden her to go out in the first place. I was crazy about that creature but well aware of her strong will.

We stood there in silence, all of us waiting.

Another minute passed as we scanned the dark forest ahead, but nothing moved other than a few leaves rustling in the evening breeze.

My stomach tightened. The anticipation was killing me.

Then a twig cracked, and Anjani pierced through the bushes like a silver arrow, her feet barely touching the ground. She ran fast as the three Destroyers slithered out of the woods, hot on her trail.

She passed the shield and crashed into me. I caught her and held her tightly, as relief washed through me.

The Destroyers tried to follow but rammed into the invisible wall. The force of the impact knocked them backward. They tumbled through the grass, cursing and hissing.

"Come here, you little rat!" one of them spat.

He got up and started punching the shield with no effect whatsoever.

The succubi laughed and cheered as they gathered around us. Anjani squealed with joy as she hugged her sisters, one by one, before they all fused into a group hug and caught me in the middle.

I chuckled and took a step back, giving them the space they needed for their reunion.

"I'm so proud of you," Anjani told one of her sisters. "You followed Hansa's signs and found us! Well done!"

"For a second there, I thought it was all some sort of twisted joke," the succubus replied. "We got here, and all we could see was an area surrounded by Destroyers. I thought someone had faked the message, sending us to our deaths!"

"Yeah, it's not that easy to find," Anjani chuckled.

I watched her as she interacted with what was left of her tribe. Her skin glowed gently, a sign of intense emotions. It warmed me, seeing her so happy, so relieved to see some of her family had survived the Destroyers' and Sluaghs' atrocious attack.

I wished Anjani could glow all the time. She was stunning when she was this happy.

14

SERENA

"Tritones," Draven repeated the word. "Interesting creatures, quite rare."

"That's what you think," the young Tritone in front of me smirked, without taking his azure eyes off me.

I moved my arms and legs, putting some distance between us in the water. My instincts were on high alert. Despite the Tritones' beautiful features, I feared that something dark and deadly lurked beneath.

"You shouldn't be afraid," another Tritone said. "Unless you mean to harm us."

I looked at him and noticed he was older but with similar physical traits—the long blond hair, the light blue eyes, the dashing smile. They all seemed to be related, sharing the same physiognomy. The only clear differentiator was in the color of their tails and fins.

"We come in peace," Draven replied, lifting his hands above the water.

"More like landed. We landed in peace," Sverik added nervously, his eyes darting around. He put on a faint smile.

I sensed a whiff of fear coming from him, a thin pale ribbon. Something told me he wasn't comfortable surrounded by so many Tritones, while Draven was perfectly calm and relaxed. I decided to follow the Druid's emotions.

"Well, then," the young Tritone said. "Let's get you out of the water first, before your fingers get all pruned. You land animals get funny when wet."

He vanished below, and I saw his orange and white tail move as he reached the shore. He used his hands to pull himself forward onto the white sand. It was the first time I noticed his belt, wrapped just below his waist where his fish tail began. It consisted of thick braided strings, a multitude of shells, and a strip of white fabric resembling organza. As he came in contact with the dry strip of sand, his tail shimmered, the colors faded away, and it split in two.

My jaw dropped as I watched his tail turn into a pair of perfectly functional legs. He stood up and waved at us. The merfolk back home definitely couldn't do *that*.

"Come on! We don't bite!" He laughed as he motioned us to follow.

Other Tritones followed him to the shore, where they, too, stood on their newly formed legs. Most, however, stayed in the water, eyeing us suspiciously. I had a feeling we had yet to earn their trust. My mind was still blocked by the fact that they could switch from fish tail to legs so easily. The Tritones had taken the notion of amphibious to a whole new level. They were like mer-shifters.

Draven, Hansa, Sverik, and I swam toward him and walked the last few feet before we reached the shore. I looked around, taking it all in. It was a breathtaking view, with tall trees casting their shadows over the turquoise water, which was crystal clear on a bed of white sand. It seemed the perfect spot for a summer vacation. It was quiet and secluded, the poster-image of sandy shores and coconut drinks in the sun.

The young Tritone who had nudged me around in the water came forward as my boots sank into the sand. He offered me his hand, and I took it. He helped me farther away from the water. Several Tritones followed.

"First and foremost, some introductions are in order," he said. "I am Zeriel, newly anointed King of the Blue Lagoon."

He bowed respectfully, and I instinctively bowed back. I glanced over my shoulder and saw Draven, Hansa, and Sverik do the same. I figured etiquette was not lost on the Eritopians, especially those calling themselves kings.

"I am Draven, a Dr—"

"Druid, yes," Zeriel interrupted him with a fascinated expression. "Though I'll say, I haven't seen one of your kind in a few decades at least."

Draven nodded curtly. "I may be the last of my kind, but I can't say for sure. This world has many excellent hiding places.

Such as this one. I'm surprised Azazel hasn't made a move on you yet. Where are we?"

The Tritones looked at each other, frowns passing over their faces.

"You don't know where you are?" Zeriel asked incredulously. "Then how did you get here?"

"Through that." I pointed at the obsidian stone on the ledge high above us.

"You came through the stone?" He clearly had trouble processing the information. "How is that possible? Magic, perhaps?"

"Wow. You guys have had a passage stone in your backyard for who knows how long, and you didn't even know it?" Hansa chuckled.

Draven shot her a glance that asked her to be respectful and diplomatic with our hosts and to avoid any unnecessary arguments. Hansa's smirk instantly vanished in response, replaced by a faint and polite smile addressed to Zeriel.

"What's a passage stone? That giant lug of obsidian has been up there for over three centuries." Zeriel laughed lightly. "I wasn't even born when this thing appeared out of nowhere. The elders spoke about it, saying it had been gifted by a Druid, but no one had any details. As far as I'm concerned, this has been a sculpture in my garden for hundreds of years. Never thought it served any purpose."

"Well, it does," Draven replied. "It's an item of great power and magic. I'd be happy to share the knowledge, should you be interested in using it."

"We swim, Druid. We don't walk through stones. But continue your story. You walked through the stone and...you landed here, in my lagoon?"

"We didn't know where it would take us. We gambled with fate, and it spared us."

Zeriel nodded, acknowledging Draven's explanation. When he focused his attention on me again, his face lit up with a bright, wide smile. He wasn't being polite or friendly. He was being downright charming and making me blush.

"And you, young lady? What wonderful species brought you to our shore, and from which planet? Because you certainly aren't from around here."

"I'm Serena," I murmured. "And you're right. I'm not from around here."

"Here for business? Or pleasure?"

The way he accentuated the word pleasure drew a modest groan from Draven, who took a step forward to stand next to me. If I didn't know any better, I could've sworn I was about to watch a nature documentary about males disputing over a female.

Zeriel was quick to notice Draven's protective frame toward me, but it didn't seem to deter him at all. On the contrary, he seemed to enjoy playing with the Druid's nerves. He stepped forward as well, closing the distance between us.

I looked up, craning my neck in the process.

"She's here with me," Draven replied.

I felt his hand on the small of my back, his fingers splayed and pressing gently. Zeriel looked at him first, then at me, and tipped his head to one side.

"That's fine, Druid. I just can't help my fascination and delight when I meet a gorgeous creature who tries to influence my mind. Reminds me of the Maras, and yet, she's nothing like them." He winked at me.

He was absolutely shameless, and given the tension seeping out of Draven, it was working. I couldn't help but giggle on the inside, watching how Zeriel's advances made him simmer.

"What are you?" the Tritone asked me.

"I'm a sentry," I replied, trying to keep it short.

"And this is Hansa, of the Red Tribe," Draven interjected, introducing the succubus to change the flow of the conversation.

"And I am Sverik, son of Arid."

"What a gang you've put together, Druid!" Zeriel remarked with amusement.

"One does what one can, given the circumstances."

"So, since you're here, would you like to join us for dinner? My brothers have just returned with a fresh catch. We'll even cook it for you!" the Tritone offered.

"I'm afraid there is no time for feasts, King of the Blue Lagoon," Draven replied. "We need help to fight against Azazel. It's why we risked traveling through the passage stone in the first place."

I could sense a faint wariness emanating from the Tritones, most likely caused by the mention of Azazel's name.

Zeriel swiftly dismissed the request but maintained his jovial demeanor. "We don't bother with mainland troubles. "We belong to the waters."

"So, what? You think you're exempt from Azazel's expansion plans?" Hansa scoffed. "Where do you think he'll go once he's done with the mainland?"

When the Tritone went silent, I chimed in.

"What do you think is going to happen, Zeriel? Azazel will need the waters. He will put out ships. He will claim ownership and control over each drop of water because it's in his nature. It's what he does. Will you succumb and swear fealty to him? Or will you stand up and fight?"

"What do you know about fighting?" Zeriel spat. "About war? About Azazel? We were the first to signal that there was something wrong with him, that his nefarious plans would doom the entire galaxy one day. We warned the Druids and were swiftly dismissed. Told to mind our waters and leave the mainland business to them. And where are they now, pray tell?"

"Dead," Draven replied bluntly. "They were foolish. We both agree on that. But there's no time for pointing fingers now. Azazel is moving on the last citadel soon, after which he will set his sights on the waters. We can defeat him. We can form an alliance and hit him with everything we have."

Zeriel didn't take his gaze off me as he spoke. His eyes narrowed.

"And what do you have, other than a Druid, an incubus, a succubus, and a sentry?" he asked.

"Three Oracles and the Daughters' guidance," I shot back.

His eyes widened, and he gasped.

I didn't have any patience left for trying to prove ourselves worthy of someone's attention. We had the power. We had the will and the determination to fight and win this. All they had to do was jump on board. Pleading would get us nowhere.

"You have Oracles?" Zeriel asked.

I nodded.

He mulled this over, most likely weighing all the options.

"Deep down I've known for a long while that it's only a matter of time before Azazel sets his eyes on our waters," he mumbled.

"Time is running out," Draven added. "Will you let your people die then? Or worse, become a snake's slaves, or will you be the king they deserve and rise up and fight?"

The question set something off in Zeriel—the ego of a ruler was always a good gamble when one wished to illicit a reaction, and Draven had played the king card perfectly. The Tritone's expression changed into something that radiated pride and determination—the kind that led entire armies to war, hell bent on victory.

"I just didn't want my people to go fight this alone after the mainland rejected our concerns. But seeing you here, complete with Oracles and the will to fight, it's something I'm willing to get behind," Zeriel announced.

He raised his arms from his sides and grinned. "What do you need from us, then?"

"To fight when we ask you to fight," Draven replied.

"Will you be fighting with us, Serena?" Zeriel looked at me.

"Of course. It's my family and friends Azazel's after. We have a score to settle."

"Good. Then I'm in."

He looked around, as if waiting for his Tritones to express the same level of enthusiasm, but he was met with raised eyebrows and scoffs. He didn't like their reaction, judging by his irritated grimace.

"We could use some excitement around here. Let's all admit it!" Zeriel addressed his people.

Some sighed. Others nodded. But the consensus was pretty much the same—they were on board with us, just not that excited about it. Only Zeriel was ecstatic.

"In that case, Druid, we need to arrange a meeting. All of us. Not just you and me and the lovely maiden." He winked at me, activating a twitch in Draven's jaw. "I can rally more creatures. There are plenty of rogue souls out there who will fight against Azazel if they know they won't be on their own."

Draven, Sverik, and Hansa looked at each other, nodding in agreement.

"First, we need to reach out to an incubus settlement on the northwestern shore of Antara," Draven replied.

"Antara?" I asked, unfamiliar with the name.

"It's the continent on which the mansion is. There are three on this planet, of which two are inhabitable. Antara and Marton. Sequeb is uninhabitable to most of us, a vast desert without a single drop of sweet water. Marton is pretty much the same, but it was blessed with a river crossing it from north to south," Draven explained briefly.

"You are still on Antara, Druid," Zeriel interjected. "But now that you mention Sequeb and Marton, I'll make sure to send scouts out there as well. There may be creatures there willing to rise against Azazel."

Draven nodded, his gaze darting from Zeriel to me. The Tritone had once again shortened the distance between us, his arm brushing against mine. Given how he behaved, he'd likely seen Draven's reaction and had decided to try and make the Druid snap. I didn't want to be there when the snap happened.

I felt him wet and cold, and it sent shivers down my spine. The Tritone was more fish than man.

He sensed my discomfort and took a step back. He was respectful at least, despite his rampant playfulness. I had to give him credit.

"This is good news," Sverik mused. "How far would you say we are from the northwestern coast? Are we even on the same side of the continent?"

"Yes, you are," Zeriel replied. "It's a couple of days' trip by foot. But we can give you one of our canoes, and it will take you close enough in a matter of hours, leaving just a few miles to the settlement."

"You know its location?" Draven asked.

"Not myself, personally. But I will take you to a Mara city. They know where it is. Besides, they're worth talking to as well regarding this alliance. Their mind-bending abilities are, well, mind-bending."

I couldn't help but smile. I liked Zeriel. For a king, there was this childish nuance about him that made him charming and fun. I could see us becoming friends in the future...provided we survived Azazel.

"I will get the canoe ready for you," he added and snapped his fingers.

Two Tritones from behind nodded and immediately jumped into the water, their legs shifting back to long beautiful fish tails as soon as they were submerged.

"Thank you, Zeriel," Draven said. "It takes all of us to make this happen. There's no guaranteed win, but it beats hiding from the monster and waiting to die."

Zeriel nodded in response, smiling. "I understand, Druid. I just wasn't aware that there was a resistance happening. Now! About that meeting! Who will you call to attend?"

"The incubus settlement I told you about is connected all over the planet. The Dearghs are in, and so are the Lamias, along with whatever incubi and succubi we can gather ourselves."

"Oh my. You got the Lamias involved?" the Tritone sounded surprised. "How'd you manage that?!"

Draven and I looked at each other in a moment of awkward silence before he responded. "We made a deal," he muttered.

Zeriel looked at us with a raised eyebrow, followed by a smirk. "Something tells me it was a pricey deal," he quipped, and my stomach churned. "Nevertheless, they've got some magic up their sleeves, and they are cruel and fierce, perfect on the battlefield. Well done!"

"Who can you bring into the fold?" Draven steered the conversation away from the Lamias.

"The Maras, who you will shortly meet. Plus a few other groups I've got in mind. Rest assured, Druid. I will make a good contribution to this alliance. Besides, we will be fighting as well, when the time comes. What we need to do now is agree on a meeting place for leaders and representatives of all those involved to discuss the terms and timeline of this alliance. Have you thought of one yet?"

We all shook our heads. We were still in the stages of wondering who to ask for help.

"I'll make a suggestion then. The northern waterfall of Mount Agrith. Destroyers don't dare get close to that mountain, since it's the birthplace of the Daughters, and even they don't have the courage to poke the pink-haired bear, if you catch my drift...and it's easy to reach from all points of Antara, including water lands, since it's the only waterfall to pour into a river that spills out into the ocean."

Draven thought about it for a long second, while Hansa and Sverik looked at each other, then at me. I could tell from their expressions that they weren't opposed to the idea.

"That makes sense," Draven ultimately replied. "Let's all

gather there, then. How long will you need to rally your people?"

"Give us seven moons from tonight. We'll swim up to Mount Agrith and make sure it's nice and secluded for a lengthy and constructive conversation. Destroyers may not dare to venture near it, but there are plenty of other spies and traitors that may be lurking around. Call it preemptive action." Zeriel cocked his head and smiled.

Draven nodded and offered his hand to shake on it. The Tritone took it and held it firmly, his eyes locked on the Druid's.

I let my sentry nature out for a minute to get a feel for what was moving between them as far as emotions went. I sensed fear and reservation but also hope and determination. None of us fully trusted each other in this lagoon, but we were all we had against a common and deadly enemy, and that was enough to build a bridge that could hold us.

Zeriel clapped his hands once, as a small canoe was pushed along the water onto the shore.

"Great stuff!" he declared. "Now, let's get you on a boat and take you to the Maras. You can speak to them first, and they'll guide you to the incubi settlement!"

"How do they know where it is? It's supposed to be quite secret," Sverik replied.

"The Maras know everything and everyone moving around their territory, incubus," Zeriel shot back, his voice solemn and heavier than usual. He was going for the extra drama in that statement, and I once again smiled on the inside. He was quite the character.

We all stepped toward the canoe. Hansa was the first to notice something off about it.

"When's the last time someone used this?" she asked, staring at it.

It looked at least a few hundred years old. The wood was cracked and worn out, the victim of unforgiving water and time. I wasn't even sure it could hold one of us, let alone four.

"It's... It's been a while," Zeriel replied. "Why?"

"I don't think it will hold us," I chimed in.

It was a miracle it was still floating, as far as I could tell.

"Don't underestimate her. She can hold her own plus the four of you quite elegantly," the Tritone replied, apparently insulted. "Looks aren't everything, you know? I mean, look at me. I'm gorgeous, but there's more to me than all this refined handsomeness. Right, Serena?"

I chuckled, unable to hold it in any longer. He cracked me up and drove Draven crazy. Both wins, in my book.

"Besides, we'll swim by your side. Someone needs to show you where the Maras' city is, anyway. Worst case scenario, the canoe breaks, and I get to hold you all the way to your destination. There's no sad ending to this story, believe me." He winked.

I looked at Draven, and, aside from his obvious irritation with Zeriel, I sensed relief. His gaze moved between the canoe and me. He let out a long torturous sigh.

"He's pulling your leg, Serena. This is no ordinary canoe," he grumbled and swiftly got in.

He reached a hand out to me, and I took it reluctantly—that dingy didn't look safe, no matter what the Druid said. But, much to my surprise, the moment I set my foot in it, I realized what he was talking about.

It was sturdy and solid on the inside, nothing like its crackled exterior. It felt reliable. There was something weird about it, some sort of magic involved. I was willing to bet on it.

We all got in, fitting comfortably, and the Tritones pushed us out across the lagoon and into a wide open ocean. Sverik and Draven rowed, and our new allies swam along with us as we headed north along the coast.

"Do you think the Maras will be interested in this alliance?" I asked Zeriel, who was swimming on his back with his upper body above the water and arms crossed under his head like he was lounging. He beamed at me as if I were the most interesting creature in the world.

"They might. And, then again, they might not. They've been fine on their own, somehow keeping Azazel's minions away from their city, but you're offering a solution to the bigger problem. You'll just have to persuade them," he replied.

I began to think about how we could do such a thing. From what Draven had told me, not much was known about the Maras, as they kept mostly to themselves and kept their distance from other species. They were known for their ability to influence minds, but other than that, they were a mystery. All

I knew was that I needed to avoid direct eye contact, based on what had happened to Jovi during their visit to Sarang Marketplace.

15

JOVI

We brought the succubi into the mansion, giving them four of the spare rooms on the ground floor. After they washed up, rinsed their leather garments, then slipped into some of the many clothes we'd gathered from the attic, we all sat down for a late dinner.

We spoke for hours, bringing each other up to speed about the plan going forward. We told them about the need to strengthen the alliance by bringing more potential allies into the fold, while they told us about the attack on the Red Tribe and how they'd survived and made their way back to the camp to find Hansa's message.

"We couldn't see anything when we got here," the succubus named Olia recounted. "We'd begun to question the authenticity of the message left behind by Hansa, but no one outside the Red Tribe can write or read our coded language." She paused, gazing around. "This truly is a remarkable place."

"I'm just happy to see you here," Anjani said. She beamed, filled with affection toward her sisters. "You're safe now. That's all that matters."

"For how long, though?" Perra replied. "With Azazel taking an interest in this house, it may be just a matter of time before he finds a way in."

"Up until a day ago, I would've disagreed," Vita interjected, her voice low and tinged with worry. "But after my vision, I'm not so sure anymore."

When the succubi looked at her with confusion, Vita briefly told them about her vision of Destroyers invading the mansion. It was enough to set Olia into action mode. She stood up, looking across the table at Anjani.

"Then we can't just sit here and do nothing!" she said.

"We're waiting for Hansa's return," Anjani replied. "They've gone out through the passage stone to look for help. Once she's back, we'll figure out the next steps."

"What about the alliance?" Olia replied, resuming her seat. "Who's in so far?"

"Us, to begin with," Anjani said. "The Dearghs and the Lamias. That's what we have so far."

"Well, that explains the snakes trotting around the house!" Perra scoffed, referring to Tamara and Eva. They didn't like each other very much. To be fair, none of us were fond of the two Lamias, but we needed their help, so we had to play nice.

"They're our allies, now," Anjani cajoled her. "We have to be good to them."

Perra sighed and nodded.

I couldn't help but marvel at Anjani's influence over her sisters. They were more or less the same age, and yet they all looked up to her with the same reverence that they'd shown toward Hansa. She had the respect normally reserved for leaders, and it said something. I felt a tingle of pride as I watched her tell the succubi about other potential allies to look for across Eritopia.

"There are plenty of other rogues out there, hiding in the woods, the swamps, and even the deserts," she mused. "Many who are most likely willing to rise against Azazel, provided they don't have to do it alone. They're survivors, not suicidal. If they know we're gathering an army, they're sure to jump in."

"Do you know where these rogues might be?" Aida asked.

"I'll show you the map later. There are certain regions where Destroyers haven't ventured yet or at all. Chances are we'll find some souls out there."

As they expanded on the issue and potential allies, I leaned back in my chair and listened quietly. My gaze was fixed on Anjani—her gestures, her facial expressions, the way she smirked when someone asked a question she already had a good answer to—they all told me that she would, one day, restore the glory of the Red Tribe. She didn't follow a path made by someone else. She led, and she carved her way through stone if she had to, in order to get what she wanted. I loved that about her.

My hand slipped into my pocket without me realizing it. My fingers played with the wolf's head pendant. My heart ached at the sight of her, and, with all my willingness to fight against what Vita had predicted, I couldn't help feeling myself torn apart on the inside each time my mind wandered back to the notion of never seeing Anjani again.

I clutched the pendant, another wave of determination coming over me as the old fae's words echoed in the back of my head. As I watched Anjani engaged in conversation, I wondered how this relationship could work between us. One probable future wanted me dead, and even if I managed to prove it wrong, how would Anjani and I work?

Who would follow whom to which realm, in order to be together? Would I convince her to come back to The Shade with me? Or would I leave everything behind and live here with her? She had a tribe to take over one day. And I was a male, the very concept traditionally rejected by succubi tribes. Those who followed the path of love left their tribes behind. Would Anjani do that? Did she feel all that for me?

A thousand questions darted around my head. I held the pendant and realized, with each moment that passed, that I had become tied to Anjani on a much deeper level. There was something growing between us, something sweet and intense that hadn't been there before—something that made me think that maybe, just maybe, I'd already found the new owner of the fae's pendant; her hair was long and curly and ink black, her eyes were the color of emeralds and gold bound together, and she was sitting right next to me.

16

AIDA

When morning came, Vita, Phoenix, Field, and I met outside in the garden, beneath the Daughter's magnolia tree. We'd left everyone else inside over breakfast. The succubi, Jovi, and Anjani looked over a map of our temporary home planet, Calliope, to identify potential hiding places for rogues and army deserters to reach out to. The Daughter was somewhere in the back garden or the greenhouse, studying flowers based on one of the atlases from Draven's study.

I'd seen Tamara and Eva lounging in a study room upstairs, browsing through books and journals, looking perpetually bored. They weren't happy to be here and stuck like the rest of us. I couldn't help but sympathize. I would've given anything to get out for a while and see the rest of this world. Vita and Phoenix felt the same. I could tell from their moods. They were getting tired of the mansion and the limited exterior space.

Field was already restless indoors, and it had only been a day since he'd last been out. I felt sorry for him, but I would rather see him cooped up than hunted by Destroyers.

The three of us sat down at the base of the magnolia tree, crossing our legs and facing each other in a triangle. We'd talked about getting together for another round of visions, with Field there, to the side, ready to jot down as many runes as possible in the process. We needed help with that, and he needed to be out of the house.

"Okay, so how do we do this?" Phoenix asked, looking around.

Destroyers and green fireflies had become a permanent part of the landscape beyond the protective shield, and we had to be as far away from their presence as possible to concentrate.

"I think we just need to focus and induce our states as usual. We close our eyes, take a few deep breaths, and go looking for specific information," I replied, and Vita nodded.

"We can't let these monsters draw our attention. We've come so far with our abilities. Letting them get to us would mean they've already won," she added.

"On the count of three, we go for a deep submersion," I said.

One, two, three.

I closed my eyes and focused on my breathing—in and out, until I lost count and found myself in a dark space with flickers of moving images in the corners of my eyes and sounds racing past me. I thought about the Destroyers and Azazel's hold on them. I focused on it as the subject of my incursion, and the darkness began to dissolve around me.

I found myself standing in a black marble chamber with green lit torches. I was once again deep in Azazel's castle here, on the planet Calliope. There was a large table in the middle with maps and lead figurines molded in the shape of soldiers strategically placed on top of them.

Patrik leaned against it, heaving and sweating and gasping for air. His large snake tail flailed around the chamber, knocking down chairs, while his upper body trembled and his muscles twitched. From what I could tell, he was struggling against something.

He groaned and leaned forward, opening his eyes. I was surprised to see them glowing green, like Azazel's torches and fireflies, not a usual color on Patrik.

"Get...out...of my head!" he hissed and shook his head.

He suffered like that for a while, and I pitied him. I stepped forward to get a better look, watching as he struggled with whatever was straining him.

"I can do this," he gasped. "I can do this."

He took a few deep breaths and closed his eyes again. Several minutes later, his breathing had become even, and his trembling had subsided. Beads of sweat dripped off him. He seemed to have regained his composure.

When his eyes peeled open, it was my turn to gasp, as they'd returned to their usual flat yellow with narrow black pupils. He blinked a couple of times, and I noticed the color changing again, this time to a very normal shade of steely blue, as if he was close to morphing back into a Druid.

His tail cracked, the horrible sound of a bone breaking. Patrik collapsed on the cold, wet floor in agonizing pain. He slammed his fist into the marble, cracking it and cursing under his breath.

"I can do this!" he growled. He returned to controlled breathing to overcome the pain.

I realized then what Patrik was trying to do. He'd found a way to get his body and mind to go against Azazel's consuming spell, and he was fighting it in an attempt to transform back to full Druid form. It occurred to me then that perhaps the Destroyer form was not completely irreversible, and I decided to follow Patrik in future visions to determine whether he would succeed in breaking the spell.

He caved in this time, the pressure and the pain too much for him to handle. His body shook to the point of violent convulsions. He gave up and cried out, tears streaming down his cheeks. His eyes flickered green again and then switched to his regular snaky yellow.

"I'll get you out of me, Azazel...I will," he spat.

He pulled himself up, holding on to the table for balance as his tail pushed him into a standing position. A knock sounded at the door.

"What?!" he barked out.

In came Marchosi, who had succumbed to Azazel's spell and was permanently stuck between Druid and serpent as a

Destroyer. He was dark, and his yellow eyes were tame, nearly lifeless. It didn't take a genius to understand just how miserable he was. His will was utterly defeated.

"What do you want?" Patrik muttered as Marchosi slithered into the room with his head down.

"I was told you wanted to speak to me."

"Ah, yes," he nodded, remembering something. "Your citadel will not give in, even without a Druid to protect them. I've tried doing things the peaceful way, but the military won't accept any of the offers I've made."

A moment passed before Marchosi responded. "Why am I here?" was his tired reply.

"An example must be made out of them. We do not tolerate rebellions or resistance, and we stomp them out before they become a rampant disease threatening the stability of Azazel's great empire." Patrik recited the words mechanically with zero conviction. "Lead a charge and wipe them all out. Take as many Destroyers with you as you need. By dawn, your city must burn."

The request took Marchosi by surprise. His eyes bugged. "You can't be serious," he replied.

"It's an order. Obey," Patrik said bluntly.

Marchosi balled his hands into fists at his sides, the muscles on his arms twitching. He was furious, glaring at Patrik as if he would've loved nothing more than to slit his throat. All that viciousness seemed to ooze out of him through each pore.

"You can't send me against my own city. You've reduced me

to this monstrosity already. You can't do this to me. I can't kill my own people!"

"You can and you will!" Patrik's voice thundered through the room.

Marchosi took a deep breath and looked away, seeming smaller all of a sudden. Patrik was not an ordinary Destroyer. From what I'd learned about him, he was a vicious and ruthless warrior who did not respond well to disobedience.

"You obey, or your head leaves your shoulders, Marchosi. There is no other option," he added, his tone dropping lower still.

They spent several minutes staring at each other before Marchosi eventually nodded and left the chamber, slamming the door behind him.

I caught a glimpse of Patrik crumbling, tears rolling down his cheeks, before the darkness took me away.

PHOENIX

M y vision took me to a strange place. I stood on the edge of a massive platform carved into a white marble wall on the side of a mountain. It was surrounded by lush green pine forests beneath a pale blue sky. There were two small moons in the sky, and dusk settled over the region.

I understood then that I wasn't on Calliope anymore, which only had one moon.

I turned around and saw a large temple that rose against the mountain, carved from the same white marble. Titanic statues of Greek-like sculptural art served as pillars—twenty of them— holding the roof up and standing atop a dozen stairs.

Large metal bowls held bright burning fires, lighting the main entrance.

I heard booming noises in the distance. Looking over my shoulder, I saw flames swallowing an entire city just a few miles away from the mountain. Explosion after explosion pierced through the sky followed by a familiar hissing sound. I used my True Sight to discover Destroyers—dozens of them—riding their winged horses, setting fires and killing people left and right. I felt queasy for a moment, before my attention was called back to the temple.

I heard feet shuffling and mumbled orders, as about ten young boys ran outside and nearly flew down the stairs followed by two older men. The boys were draped in white silks, similar to Roman togas. They wore gold belts and had bare arms with three to six ring tattoos each. They were Druids, as were the elders guiding them. The elders were dressed in crimson red silks of a similar fashion, and their arms were covered in Druid tattoos.

"Hurry up, boys!" one of the old Druids urged. "They'll be here any second!"

There were winged horses waiting on the edge of the platform, just where the woods started. The young Druids jumped in the saddles, two per horse. They seemed scared, their eyes darting all around.

"Masters, what will you do?" a teenage Druid asked, his eyebrows drawn into a concerned frown.

"We will hold them off," the other old one replied. "Remember, keep your heads down and fly as far north as possible! You'll recognize the shelter when you see it! Jasmine will wait for you there!"

"You must come with us!"

"There is no time! Someone needs to keep the monsters here and away from you! Our legacy is in your hands now. Preserve it and make your ancestors proud, for the day will come when you will be needed to rise against Azazel and reclaim the twenty thrones to restore peace!"

The hissing sounded closer this time, and I couldn't help but root for the young Druids to make it out of there alive.

"Go!" the first Druid barked, slapping a horse's rump. The creature neighed and took off, followed by the other four. Their wings stretched, spanning a few yards each, and flapped several times before they became dots and faded into the night sky.

The old Druids were right. Barely minutes after the boys flew away, Destroyers invaded the platform, slipping off their giant horses and slithering toward them, swords drawn. They grinned, their eyes glowing green as they bared their fangs and attacked the Druids.

Blue flames jumped out of one Druid's hands, swallowing a Destroyer whole, moments before a poisoned spear shot through him. Within seconds, he collapsed, writhing in pain and foaming at the mouth. He died in agony.

The other Druid put up a fight as well, casting energy pulses outward that knocked the Destroyers back. By the time the creatures got back into an upright position, the Druid had already disappeared inside the temple. I followed, along with the Destroyers.

"Come out, Derion. You know you can't hide from us. Not in

here!" one of the monsters shouted, his deep voice echoing through the building.

The interior of the temple was superb—most likely centuries of craftsmanship had gone into it for it to look the way it did. Hundreds of finely sculpted columns with intricate details supported the arched ceiling, which opened in the middle to reveal thousands of stars in the night sky above.

Just below that was a small gold platform holding a pulpit draped in red silk with gold embroidery that depicted swirling snakes and trees. A large book had been left open on top. This was a study hall, filled with wooden benches placed around the pulpit.

Myriads of candles were mounted all over the hall, glazing the place in a warm amber light.

As soon as the Destroyers stormed in, they snickered and spread out, looking for the old Druid named Derion.

"Come on, old boy. Where'd you hide the kids? Azazel wants them," another Destroyer yelled as he threw several benches aside.

"You brought shame to our entire species," the Druid's voice echoed around the hall. "I allowed you in here to learn and honor Eritopia and its bountiful nature, and you soiled it when you became Azazel's toy soldiers!"

The Destroyers hissed as they searched for the old Druid, but he was nowhere to be found. It was then that I recognized Goren among the attackers, bulky and tall and filled with hate.

His eyes were yellow. His fists yanked a bench up and threw it over the others.

The wood broke and splintered and scattered across the floor.

"Come out here, you ancient fool, and fight me! Or are you scared?" Goren spat, looking around.

He squinted. His gaze settled on a large painting mounted against a wall, flanked by two large bookcases. It depicted a brave Druid with a spear vanquishing a giant snake; it seemed like an allegory of sorts, of the Druid conquering his snake nature.

"You have no respect for this world and for yourselves, to allow Azazel to turn you into the monsters you've become. You've lost your magic so you can serve him. I'm surprised the Grand Temple hasn't collapsed on itself from your dirty presence," the Druid's voice boomed.

Goren grinned and threw his spear into the painting. Its poisoned tip pierced the canvas precisely where the painted hero's heart would have been. A muffled thud was heard behind it, before the painting fell forward and revealed a secret passage. The old Druid had been hiding there and was now lying dead on the floor, spear half through his chest and blood pooling around him.

"You talk and talk, and you forget we know this place as well as you do, old fool," Goren smirked, then waved at the other Destroyers. "Search every inch of this place, all the way into the catacombs! The little brats are here somewhere!"

The Destroyers obeyed, scattering around the hall and disappearing through the many doors and the passage where Derion lay dead.

"Take them alive," Goren added. His voice faded as I slipped from the vision.

18

VITA

I was on a set of black marble stairs. I heard movement at the bottom.

Phoenix ran past me up the stairs, followed by Aida and the future version of me. We looked terrible. Our clothes were ripped and blood had dried on our arms.

I ran after us and reached the top. My heart stopped as I recognized the platform—the obsidian structure with arches and pillars. Broken glass spheres were scattered across the black shiny floor. I was once again standing atop Luceria, Genevieve's former residence taken over by Azazel.

The scene I witnessed was something out of a movie. Everything seemed to move at a much slower pace, as if someone was playing it in slow motion.

The sky above was dark, with gray clouds billowing and flashing all over.

Phoenix, Aida, and future me were at the top of the stairs, and I stood right next to them as we saw Destroyers slithering up after us. Phoenix pushed a barrier out, knocking them down. They fell backward and tumbled down the stairs, their voices intertwined with others. I heard swords clanging and groans and thuds.

I looked back up at the platform and saw Serena on the floor a few yards away. She was holding Draven in her arms. He'd been injured severely. Blood trickled out of a deep stomach wound. His eyes were closing slowly as Serena called out his name repeatedly, trying to keep him conscious.

Jovi was fighting Marchosi, their swords clashing as they moved about. Jovi was swift and quick on his feet, but the Destroyer was a worthy opponent and the only one left standing between Jovi and Azazel, who stood at the center of the platform, grinning with satisfaction. Destroyers' bodies were scattered around, along with several incubi. My stomach churned as I moved around, looking for Bijarki.

"I told you before, little children, that you cannot and will not do anything to stop this from happening. Eritopia is mine, and you are but bugs in need of squashing." Azazel's voice boomed like thunder.

His veins were swollen and glowing green. He breathed heavily, and, judging by the pained shadows flickering across his face, he wasn't feeling too great. But he was still standing, his tail twitching, the snake pendant moving with its ruby eyes against his broad chest.

"Your Destroyers are all dead," Phoenix shot back, walking toward him.

Aida jumped in to help her brother, picking a sword up off the ground. The wolf siblings were truly fierce together, even when facing a foe as large and as vicious as Marchosi, with his glowing green eyes and bared fangs. He brought his sword down over and over again.

"But my power isn't, little Oracle," Azazel replied.

Several incubi made it to the top of the stairs, one of them taking future me in a brief embrace. A wave of relief washed over me as I recognized Bijarki. He looked around, then drew his bow and arrow, shooting one straight at Azazel.

It stopped midair as Azazel raised his palm against it. With a flick of his fingers, the arrow turned back and shot right through Bijarki's shoulder, throwing him backward. Future me screamed and caught Bijarki before he fell over the edge to his death and pulled him back up.

"You won't win, Azazel, no matter what tricks you've got left up your sleeves. You are nothing without your Destroyers, just a failed Druid with a bunch of spells against thousands of creatures who want you dead and out of this world." Phoenix took another step forward, fists closed at his sides.

I heard another thud and saw Marchosi on the ground, both Jovi and Aida's swords stuck in his neck, his spinal cord severed. They both stood over him, watching as he gave his last breath.

"You little bugs have yet to understand who I am," Azazel

replied and stretched his arms outward as more clouds gathered above him, circling and thundering menacingly.

A pink shimmer appeared out of nowhere on the edge of the platform, several yards away from Azazel, who was now the last Destroyer standing.

Current me realized then that we'd get very far in our fight against him, and that glimmer of a potential victory reignited my hope when I needed it the most.

I glanced over at future me and saw Bijarki still breathing, though injured. The look in his eyes spoke of love, and my heart fluttered for a moment, before I shifted my focus back to the pink shimmer. It flashed and threw sparks around before it shaped itself into the last Daughter.

Phoenix stilled, his eyes wide and mouth gaping.

"You're okay," he gasped.

Azazel froze. His mouth turned into a thin line.

"I couldn't stay away anymore," the Daughter replied with a weak smile. "My sisters sent me."

Phoenix sighed and moved toward her, but the Daughter raised her palm in the air, motioning him to stop. She then looked at Azazel, her smile fading.

"It's time to stop this," she said.

"What are you doing here?" Azazel hissed furiously. "I thought I told you ladies to stay away or the little one gets it!"

A powerful wind began to blow, lifting loose fabrics and strands of black dust from the floor. Thunders boomed above, increasing in intensity and volume.

The sound of war unraveled below, and I looked over the ledge to see Dearghs and an army of creatures engaged in a siege of the castle. Flames shot across the crowds and exploded into the gates. Wood splintered, and stone bricks crumbled. It hit me then that I was watching the same scene I'd previously seen with Hansa and Anjani but from a different angle—the top of Azazel's castle.

My stomach shrank into a tiny but heavy ball as I saw the Daughter's eyes light up in a fluorescent violet. The wind blew through her hair, raising wave upon wave of reddish pink strands over her shoulders. She wore a white translucent dress that glimmered with diamonds. The fabric fluttered as brutal gusts swept around her bare feet. Thick gold bracelets hung around her ankles and wrists.

I held my breath as I watched drops of liquid gold seep through the skin on her pale face, taking the form of a gold mask, similar to the ones I'd seen the other Daughters wear. Her eyes shone violet, and her voice sounded like a million people speaking, the same as I'd heard earlier at the mansion when she'd spoken about Goren.

"Our little sister is out of your reach, Azazel." The Daughter's multiple voices echoed across the platform, making the obsidian floor and pillars vibrate in the process.

Azazel's face went blank.

I tried to understand what she was talking about. Was there another Daughter? Had Azazel kept her prisoner, forcing the

Daughters to stay away and not intervene as he laid waste to Eritopia's planets?

The Daughter stepped forward, prompting Azazel to move back a few feet, unsure of what to do next.

"How did that happen?" he asked incredulously.

"Well, we did tell you not to mess with us," Aida smirked, standing tall and proud next to her brother.

Azazel looked at them and pursed his lips. He moved his arm as if swatting a fly away, and shot out a pulse that crashed into Aida and Jovi, sending them flying then rolling along the floor. They slid across the smooth obsidian and nearly fell over the edge. Jovi was the first to stop. He grabbed Aida just as her legs went past the edge, dangling in the air. He pulled her back. They both took gasping breaths. Whatever Azazel had thrown at them, it had knocked the air out of their lungs.

"Azazel," the Daughter said in her creepy multiple voices, "you have committed unspeakable crimes against Eritopia, against the people, and against the Daughters themselves. You show no remorse and revel in the blood you have spilled. Today, I bring it all to an end, on behalf of my sisters and Eritopia. This world does not want you anymore, you snake."

She closed the distance between them as Azazel threw flames and pulses at her, trying to stop her advance. But nothing worked. The Daughter didn't flinch or waver. The closer she got, the paler his face became. His lower lip trembled. For the first time, I saw genuine fear in his yellow eyes.

"No, you can't," he barked. "I've gained tremendous power. You can't take me down anymore!"

She tilted her head to one side as the wind grew stronger, circling around the platform. "You have been sentenced to death by the very world that allowed your creation, Azazel. You were given a gift, and you abused it. You have soiled the very magic of your honorable heritage, the power that Eritopia blessed you with."

She raised her hand and touched his face, her veins glowing pink.

He shut his eyes tightly, as if expecting to die. I guessed it was the touch of death that Bijarki had mentioned, as the Daughters were able to kill a person just by touching them. However, it didn't kill Azazel. As a matter of fact, it didn't have any effect on him at all.

She withdrew her hand, staring at it in confusion.

Azazel gasped and grinned when he realized he was still alive. "I'm growing tired of repeating myself." He laughed maniacally. "I cannot be stopped. What will it take for you all to understand?"

He backhanded the Daughter, throwing her back a few feet. She landed on her side, mask still on her face but eyes wide open, flickering as she struggled to get back up. Phoenix jumped at Azazel almost out of sheer instinct, bringing his fist down into the Destroyer's face. Azazel's arm shot out and grabbed him by the throat, choking him as he lifted him off the ground.

"Be a good boy and go back to your glass bubble," he hissed and threw Phoenix away like a rag doll.

The Daughter stood up, her eyes glowing violet again. She watched Phoenix as he rolled on the floor, heaving and choking. She focused her attention on Azazel once more, her thousand voices ringing louder than before, to the point where I had to cover my ears.

"I see," she said. "Then so it must be, that a Daughter will sacrifice herself to rid the world of the disease that you've become."

"No!" Phoenix shouted at her, his expression livid with pain and desperation.

I saw Serena's stunned face. She clutched Draven in her arms. His eyes were closed, and his chest was no longer moving. Jovi and Aida managed to get back on their feet and run toward the Daughter, while future me held Bijarki close. We all watched in horror as Aida and Jovi failed to reach her in due time.

A blinding pink light shone out of her body, and a loud flash and bang followed as the light swallowed us all like a nuclear explosion, deconstructing every particle in its path—including us. I screamed.

I sat up screaming.

Aida and Phoenix held me, helping me regain my senses. I

broke into a cold sweat. Tears streamed down my cheeks, and I struggled to catch my breath. Field was on his knees in front of us, jotting down the last runes flitting along my arms before they vanished.

"Shh, Vita. It's okay." Aida kissed my temple.

Both she and Phoenix seemed pale, the shadows of runes fading away from their faces.

"You had a really long and intense one, didn't you?" Phoenix asked me, his voice low.

"Just one vision," I gasped. "And it was horrible."

"We had just one vision too," Aida replied. "We woke up a few minutes ago, and you were still deep under, frowning and crying and moaning. We didn't know what to do, so we waited."

"Are you okay?" Field looked at me with concern.

I nodded and wiped the tears from my eyes, gradually regaining my composure.

"I saw the end of this, of everything!" I croaked, swallowing back another wave of tears.

They sat there and looked at me as I told them the entire vision in blistering detail, from beginning to end. By the time I was done, they were as floored as I was. Phoenix was particularly devastated. His skin was pale, and beads of sweat dripped from his forehead.

We sat there for a while, as Aida and Phoenix took turns recounting their own visions. The weird part was that we'd only had one vision each, as opposed to the sets of three that we'd grown accustomed to. What did it mean, and why had it changed now?

My stomach churned as I realized I'd come out of this last vision with more questions than answers. And the most pressing of them all was how we were going to stop that massive explosion from happening.

19

PHOENIX

I'd already sensed the enormous destructive potential the Daughter had, so having it confirmed by Vita's vision only added more weight to my suspicion. Her sisters had told her that sacrifice would be required to rid this world of Azazel, and the thought of her perishing in the process shot daggers through my heart.

I sat there, listening as Aida and Vita tried to make sense of what was going to happen, as if they also had a hard time believing that it would eventually come to that. I, on the other hand, began to contemplate the prospect of my own death, not just the Daughter's. I had first-hand knowledge of the energy core she possessed and knew what that bright pink blast described by Vita meant. No one on that platform would survive.

"Should we tell the Daughter?" Aida mumbled.

"That she may be the one to kill us all?" Vita replied with a hint of sarcasm.

"We can't just keep it from her! She might be able to prevent it all if she's told."

"And what if she just takes it as something that absolutely has to happen? What then?" Vita's skepticism wasn't misplaced, but I agreed with Aida.

"I know her," I said, my voice weak. "She wouldn't go all end-of-days on us. She doesn't want this any more than we do. We should tell her."

Vita's gaze dropped, settling on her palms. She took a deep breath and ran her fingers through her hair, nodding slowly.

"Okay, Phoenix. You'll be the one to tell her. Now, despite the fact that we've only had one vision each, we've come out with some crucial information," she said.

"Yeah, first and foremost, we're all going to die," Aida replied.

"I mean besides that. We know that there may be more Druids out there, still alive, from what Phoenix saw. Maybe during your next vision, Aida, you can focus on them, see if they're still alive."

Aida nodded. Field moved to sit next to her holding the sheets of old paper and graphite in his hands. He'd jotted down as much as he'd been able to gather from our runes. It was now up to the Daughter to interpret these messages. However, I didn't have enough patience to deal with more cryptic messages. None of the runes she'd translated so far had yielded anything clear. Just riddles and ambiguous one-liners that had yet to reveal their true meaning.

"We know that Patrik is struggling with his condition and trying to break free from Azazel's spell. We may be able to reach out to him, maybe even help him. He obviously doesn't want to be a Destroyer," Vita added.

"He just ordered the annihilation of an entire city. I doubt he'll come willingly," I replied, unable to see past the ruthless Destroyer form. In my mind, once they went dark and committed the atrocities for which they'd become notorious, they could no longer go back.

"His will belongs to Azazel, Phoenix. It's not like he has any control over it. You didn't see him. He puts himself through a lot of pain just to try to break free from it all. I can't put the full responsibility of mass murder on his shoulders, not when I know for a fact that he's fighting it, that he doesn't want it. He doesn't have a choice, but if we find a way to remove Azazel's spell, it would mean we could turn others, too," Aida explained.

"Assuming the others would want to be turned back."

"Marchosi is the same. He doesn't want to be there. He had no other choice but to say yes. I'm not sure any of us would be able do things differently if we were in his place," she replied. "What I'm saying is that we have spotted an actual weakness in Azazel's army. It's something we've never been able to glimpse before, and it could end up being the tipping point of this entire war. We could turn the tide in our favor."

What Aida said made sense, even if I didn't like it. If we

saved Patrik from his curse, we would gain his support, and, from what we'd learned so far, we knew that he was one of Azazel's most powerful lieutenants. That much strength combined with tremendous inside knowledge would surely bring us closer to defeating the monster. The fact that Azazel had not learned what Patrik was up to was another positive key point in the strategy, meaning that the lieutenant was duplicitous enough to be an effective "inside man".

"We can also assume there is another Daughter," Vita continued. "And Azazel has her. It's why the Daughters haven't intervened against him. They must have made some sort of bargain. Her life and safety for their withdrawal."

"Then why did they put this protective shield around the house? Maybe that's how the Destroyers get in, maybe Azazel holds the other Daughter over their heads and forces them to remove the shield eventually, once he figures out it's their doing? And why did they shroud Eritopia in a spell that keeps Azazel in, if he has their sister?" I asked, going over possible scenarios.

"Maybe there were terms and conditions to their agreement. Maybe the Daughters stayed away to protect their sister but found a loophole to still intervene without breaking the deal with Azazel," Field mused, looking into the distance.

I followed his gaze and saw Goren leaving a group of Destroyers behind to get closer to the shield. He looked up, his lips moving.

"I'll look into this when I go under next time," I replied. I nodded toward Goren. "What is he doing there? Talking to himself?"

Aida looked at him and was the first to stand up and approach him. We followed and reached the shield to find Goren looking pale and sweaty, mumbling as he paced around a patch of yellow grass.

"My liege, we've tried everything," he said, gazing up.

A few green fireflies flew above his head, and a deep voice echoed from them.

"*Until the explosive charges I've sent get to you, continue to keep an eye on the space,*" the voice said. "*There are creatures in it. I saw some of them before the Druid stomped us out.*"

"That's Azazel," Vita gasped. "I recognize that voice. It's him!"

"What do we do if anyone comes out, my liege?" Goren asked the fireflies. "Do we shoot to kill?"

"*Not unless you have to. I want them alive. There's a creature in there with large black wings. I want him for my collection.*"

We all looked at Field at the same time. He stilled, eyes fixed on Goren. Aida was as white as a sheet of paper as she placed her hand on his arm.

"He saw you," she managed to say, her lower lip trembling.

"Understood, my liege," Goren replied and bowed as the fireflies scattered.

The Destroyer slithered away back to the camp they'd made several yards to our right. I felt queasy at the thought of Field being on Azazel's radar.

"Field, he saw you," Aida repeated with panic in her voice.

"It's fine. I'm obviously not flying out anytime soon." His reply was calm and composed. I figured he didn't want her to worry too much. He took her in his arms and held her tight. Her head rested on his chest.

"Either way, this isn't good. I can't help but wonder how much he saw through those fireflies," Vita said, watching Goren as he left.

"And what explosive charges was he talking about?" I asked.

Was he going to try and blow the shield up? Did he know what kind of magic he was dealing with?

Would those explosives be what would eventually let the Destroyers in?

20

AIDA

W e moved our conversation inside Draven's study, behind closed doors. Field took it upon himself to scour some of the Druid's books for any information we could use, while Vita, Phoenix, and I continued looking over possible scenarios based on our visions and the choices we could make.

"Let's just remember that what Vita saw is a possible future, not an absolute certainty," Phoenix said, pacing around the room.

"True, but it's not just any possible future," I replied. "It's one that kills us all. The Daughter will explode, and we will all die. Are any of us ready to deal with our mortality? Because I am having a hard time brushing this off as a possible future. I'm sorry." My stomach twisted in knots.

Phoenix stopped to look at me with a pained expression and shook his head slowly.

"No, Aida. I'm not looking to die anytime soon, nor am I willing to let the Daughter die. Let's not forget that there's a very high chance that if she dies, I die too, no matter where I am. And that's not on my to-do list," he replied.

"We can't look at Vita's vision as something to just accept. We have to see it as something we can avoid," Field interjected, while flipping through an old almanac.

Vita collapsed in Draven's chair, shuddering and swallowing back tears. She'd actually seen it happen. She'd taken it the hardest out of all of us.

I moved to kneel before her, resting my hands on her knees in a reassuring gesture. I had to keep her calm—we all had to keep our composure if we wanted to prevent a tragedy.

"It's okay, Vita," I said gently. "Phoenix will talk to the Daughter, and we'll find a way to stop it from happening. He does have a point, as grim as that vision might have been. The Daughter would never do this on purpose. She wouldn't kill us all. She'd help us find a way to stop it, I'm sure."

The door burst open, startling us. The Daughter stood in the doorway in her white linen dress, her reddish pink hair disheveled and violet eyes glazed with tears. She'd been crying.

"I would never... I don't want to hurt you," she sobbed as more tears streamed down her cheeks. She stepped forward into the room. "I don't want to kill you. I don't want to die. I love you all so much. You've been so good to me. I can't. I just can't."

She broke down.

Phoenix reached her in two wide steps and took her in his

arms. He held her close, kissing the top of her head as she let out all her grief. His shirt muffled her voice.

I felt sorry for her and Phoenix. They'd gotten so close so quickly.

"It's okay," he said to her. "It's okay."

"But it's not! I don't want to kill anyone! I don't want to hurt anyone!"

"You heard us talking about the vision, didn't you?" Vita asked.

The Daughter looked up and nodded between hiccups. It was truly heartbreaking to see her in that condition. She was one of the most innocent creatures I'd ever seen, and watching her cry brought my own tears back to the surface.

"I was walking past the door and heard Phoenix's voice. I stopped for a minute, just to make sure he was okay, and I...I don't know much about what you saw, but if I'm meant to end it all, there has to be another way," the Daughter replied, wiping her eyes.

"In Vita's vision, you explode." Phoenix sighed. "There's a bright pink flash that wipes everything out, including Azazel. We don't know anything else beyond that."

"How do I get there with you?" the Daughter asked.

"We don't know." He shrugged. His gaze was fixed on her face, reading her expression carefully. "But apparently your presence there, on top of Azazel's castle, is a surprise to us, to me. As if you'll be gone and then returning to destroy Azazel."

"And there's another thing you should know," Vita said.

"According to my vision, Azazel has another Daughter in his possession. She's referred to as a child, the little one, and she's the reason why your sisters haven't been more active against Azazel."

The Daughter stilled. Her eyes were wide and glassy, and her lips parted slowly.

"A younger sister? How is that possible?" she asked.

"We were hoping you could tell us. Do you know or remember anything?" Phoenix asked.

"I...I don't know." She shook her head. "I wish I knew... I...I can reach out to my sisters. I can talk to them. I can visit them in my dreams, but I usually stay away, because they always tell me the same thing. That I need to wake up and take control. That I must end it all. That my sacrifice will be required to rid Eritopia of this darkness. They always make me sad and worried, so I stay away from them. But...but knowing this now, knowing that I may one day kill you all...that I have another sister and that Azazel has her... I have no choice. I have to speak to them."

We spent a minute looking at each other.

The Daughter wrapped her arms around Phoenix's waist, seeking comfort and warmth.

I had a hard time seeing her the way Vita had seen her in her vision. All I could see was a fragile young woman with powers she had yet to fully understand. Even that freaky thing she'd done with Goren, she'd had no idea how it happened or whether she could do it again. Her abilities came to her in sudden, unexpected snippets, and we'd all agreed to look after her, protect her, and help her. She'd been nothing but sweet and helpful in return.

"Are you sure it's a good idea to speak to your sisters?" Vita asked reluctantly. "Last time we reached out to them, they took Draven's eyes. They've not been exactly friendly or easy to deal with. What if they make everything worse?"

"But they also answered the succubi's prayer," I murmured, remembering my vision of Anjani's sisters around the campfire and the appearance of that strange crystal. "While we don't know what that means, we know for a fact that they're listening and that they can see what's happening across the galaxy."

"Yet they're also telling the Daughter that she has to sacrifice herself," Vita replied. "And then I see her destroying us all. I have a feeling their involvement runs deeper than we initially thought. After all, none of them bothered to mention that Azazel has their sister, so I really don't trust them. Especially after I saw Destroyers coming into the mansion. Their protective shield is supposed to keep them out."

I sighed heavily and slumped. Vita had a point. The Daughters had not been very forthcoming, nor had they been useful. Instead of answers, they gave us more riddles. Instead of help, they crippled Draven for days.

"I have to try," the Daughter mumbled.

It wasn't a comfortable idea, but we'd run out of options. There wasn't enough of that invisibility spell to get us all out of the Destroyers' range if we decided to leave the shield on foot. Field had captured Azazel's attention, which made his flight far too risky to be considered as an escape option. Worrying about Field's safety shot thousands of sharp pins through my heart.

We didn't know whether Draven, Serena, Hansa, and Sverik had made it safely onto the other side—wherever that was. I was having trouble summoning a vision of them, because why should my Oracle abilities work without a glitch, huh? And the mansion was surrounded by Destroyers who would soon be in possession of explosive charges. Adding Vita's visions of Destroyers invading the house and the Daughter obliterating us on top of it all made it even clearer.

The Daughter reaching out to her sisters wasn't the best idea, but at this point, it seemed to be all we had left.

21

SERENA

E vening had set in by the time we reached the northern shore. The ocean lapped gently at our canoe as Draven and Sverik paddled in a constant rhythm. The sky was painted in dark shades of blue and purple. Billions of stars glistened above, and the giant moon shed light on the white marble mountainside rising above the water.

Zeriel and a dozen other Tritones swam below and occasionally jumped and splashed around playfully. I sat up straight with Draven behind me. His breath tickled the back of my neck. I looked over my shoulder to find Draven's steely eyes focused on me. I smiled, and he winked in response, making me tingle all over.

His mere presence was illuminating and energizing to me, and I had a feeling that we were still barely scratching the surface of our relationship. The one thing I knew for sure was that he would be the force I needed to push through and save myself, my friends, and him. The universe had been kind enough to not drop us into a volcano when we passed through the stone. I took that as a good sign and found hope in the thought that one day our biggest worry would be deciding whether to move permanently back to The Shade or live in Eritopia with our newfound friends and lovers.

The sight before me broke my train of thought. As we got closer to the Maras' city, it proved to be a mighty fortress carved into a white marble wall. It was a simple and minimalistic structure with narrow stairs leading up and down to different levels. It had sprawling terraces, straight architectural lines, and small, square windows.

Its base opened out onto the white sandy beach. The fortress was covered with a large rectangular roof, supported by tall columns, and reached the shore via a series of low, wide steps.

"Here we are," Zeriel said, gripping the side of our canoe as he pulled us closer to the beach. "It's called White City."

"Simple, but accurate," I quipped, marveling at the enormous structure before us.

"I should warn you not to speak out of turn when we meet them, at least not before I make the introductions," the Tritone warned, his beautiful tail morphing into a pair of legs once more as he reached the shore, while the belt and delicate fabric he permanently wore around his waist served as a clothing piece.

We got out of the canoe and walked across the sand. The other Tritones followed us.

I looked up at the city, then at Zeriel, who was shamelessly admiring me, his eyes smiling.

"Are they aggressive?" I asked.

"It depends on how you come across. They're ruthless by nature but will not bother to kill you themselves. They'll bend your mind and convince you to do it yourself," he replied casually, looking over his shoulder.

I gulped.

One by one, the Maras emerged from the base of the city, seemingly floating down the stairs toward us. Their long black capes covered their bodies and heads. I couldn't see much, so I turned on my True Sight to get a better look at their faces.

"How have they survived here for so long?" Hansa asked. "Why hasn't Azazel crushed them? Better yet, why haven't they risen against him since they can control people's minds?"

"Their numbers have dwindled over the past centuries. Azazel's magic is stronger. His Destroyers aren't fully affected by the Maras' powers, from what I'm told," Zeriel replied, watching as they walked toward us. Their feet barely touched the sand. "Normally, an adult Mara can push you into doing and thinking anything, and you lose control over your will, and, in some cases, even your memory if they want you to. But I heard the Destroyers' wills already belong to Azazel, so they're not something the Maras can take. I believe they're better equipped to answer your questions in full detail, Hansa."

I scanned the Maras approaching, and the one in the middle leading the group caught my attention. His skin was pale, his eyes were the color of jade, and his features were strikingly beautiful, as if he'd been carved out of a marble block by Michelangelo himself. The others were equally superb creatures, tall and pale, their eyes in different shades ranging from black to intense greens and blues.

The middle Mara was the first to reach us. His gaze scanned us from left to right, then head to toe. I stilled when his eyes met mine and flared a most peculiar yellow, as if lights had been turned on behind the jade irises. He cocked his head to one side and took a step closer.

I felt Draven's hand brush against mine as he stepped forward in response, as if asserting himself as my protector. While I found that incredibly hot and sweet, I had a lineage to honor. I took a deep breath and introduced myself as a sentry by reaching out to the Mara's mind. I attempted to read his emotions. It was more about making my powers felt than anything else. But I hit a blank wall.

"Zeriel," the Mara said, ignoring me completely. "What brings you here?"

"We need to talk, Jax," the Tritone replied. "There's an alliance coming together against Azazel."

"And how is that my concern?"

"How is it not? Eritopia is your home too," I replied, even as I wondered why I couldn't reach out to him with my sentry abilities. He looked at me, his mouth curving upward as he pulled his hood down, revealing his short black hair.

"What are you?" he asked, then looked at Zeriel. "What is she? And what are you doing here? Unless you are here to repay the debt for Pyrope, I'm not interested in talking to you."

"Pyrope? What's Pyrope?" I questioned the Tritone, who gave us a sheepish smile.

"It's an old favor that I have to repay," he replied, then glanced at the Mara. "Can we talk about Pyrope later, please? My word is my bond. You know I'm good for it."

It took the Mara a few moments to respond. His gaze fixed on me. He nodded.

"Thank you," Zeriel replied, seeming relieved. "These are our new friends. Jaxxon, meet Draven, Hansa, Sverik, and Serena. They're here to talk to you about joining forces against Azazel. I've already agreed to participate."

"That's because you're a reckless little fool who never thinks twice before putting himself and his people in danger," Jax shot back coldly.

I looked around and noticed the hostility on the Maras' faces as they took their hoods off. They were all superb, with shortish hair—even the females. I figured it was a cultural thing and made a note to ask them later, provided this conversation led to something constructive.

"He's already in danger, and so are his people," I interjected, unwilling to let him poke my new Tritone friend. There weren't enough people who had been kind and helpful to us, so I'd quickly learned to appreciate and protect the few who were. "Azazel is about to completely destroy Eritopia. He's gaining ground everywhere, and we have to stop him. It's either that or die."

"No, but seriously, what are you?" Jax ignored my statement completely. "I know a Druid when I see one, and I'm rather tired of succubi and incubi at this point, but you...you I cannot understand. What are you?"

Hansa and Sverik scoffed almost simultaneously, and I felt tension flowing out of Draven, who didn't take his eyes off Jax. I wrapped my fingers around the Druid's wrist and squeezed gently as I smiled at Jax. I felt Draven relax slowly, trusting me to hold my own against the Mara.

"I'm what's called a sentry," I replied. "I'm not from around here."

"That's an understatement," he muttered after a pause, then took a deep breath. "But very well. Let's leave it at that. As for my disdain toward the Tritone's way of handling a war alliance, rest assured I speak from personal experience with Zeriel. He really doesn't think things through."

I noticed the guilt on Zeriel's face as he looked away. The Mara and the Tritone clearly had history, and I made it a part of my mission to find out all I could about them.

"However," Jax continued. "I'm no fool. We've been doing fine on our own here, but we are perfectly aware that our luck will soon run out. My concern is that the alliance you're proposing may not be worth our time or our lives, should we decide to put them on the line. You'd better bring something grand to the table, otherwise you will not have our support. There are few of us left, and we don't intend to mindlessly charge into battle with a handful of amateurs."

"You underestimate the abilities of the succubi, milord," Hansa replied, gritting her teeth.

Jax's gaze settled on the succubus, measuring her from head to toe. It was difficult to read his expression, as he maintained a cool composure.

"I've not met a succubus I couldn't bring to her knees in absolute obedience before she could even raise a hand against me," he shot back, his voice low. "Rest assured, until that happens, I'm not underestimating anything."

Hansa was fast—much faster than I remembered. She drew her sword and brought it up to Jax's neck. It happened in the fraction of a second, a silvery flash and a gust of air as her blade touched his skin, and she stood in front of him, her face inches from his. Jax was still, and Hansa grinned, their gazes locked on each other.

"I hope I've managed to change your mind, milord," she said.

The Mara's pupils dilated, and his eyes glowed for a moment—an incandescent amber yellow—enough to make Hansa take a few steps back. Her body trembled with each movement. She was clearly no longer in control. Jax didn't break eye contact with her until she found her place next to me, breathing heavily as the mind control kept her muscles stiff.

She was trying to fight it, her knuckles white and eyes shooting daggers at him, but the Mara didn't let go that easily.

The rest of us were frozen. Multiple scenarios ran through my head, each ending in some bloody way. The Maras were within their rights to retaliate. I raised my hand in what I hoped would be taken as a calming gesture. I didn't want to try using my sentry abilities against him again. We were trying to form a peaceful alliance, not kill each other.

"Jax, please, you've made your point," I said to him.

He kept his eyes on Hansa and smiled.

"No, she's made hers. She showed me hers. I showed her mine," he said, then looked at me.

Hansa was suddenly free, taking deep breaths and cursing under her breath as she put her sword away. She straightened her back and raised her chin proudly, and Jax nodded in return.

"Let us talk, then," he said and glanced at the Maras behind him.

They stepped aside to clear a path for us to the city. Jax went first, and we followed. I looked over my shoulder and saw all the Maras' eyes focused directly on me, occasionally glowing the same faint yellow I'd seen on Jax. Shivers ran down my spine. I wasn't sure what they wanted from me, but I had a feeling they were trying their mind-bending skills on me, like Jax had done before them, and failing, just like I'd failed to use my mind-reading abilities on their lord.

Jax guided us to a private hall that was dressed entirely in the same white marble with a smooth glossy finish. Giant candles melted in black iron chandeliers that hung from the tall, arched ceiling. We sat around a large table, and Maras served water and bowls of fruit.

Draven brought Jax up to speed regarding Azazel's advances on Eritopia and what we'd learned so far. He told him about the Oracles but kept the Daughter out of the conversation, using the same line I'd given Zeriel and stating that we had the Daughters' support. Jax sat back in his chair quietly, listening to everything that Draven had to say. He occasionally looked at Hansa, whose gaze darted around the hall analyzing each Mara who stood by the wall staring blankly ahead.

"These must be his bodyguards," Hansa mumbled next to me.

Draven continued his alliance speech. "We have the Lamias and Dearghs' support, and the Tritones have been gracious enough to join us as well. There is a rogue incubi settlement not far from here, which I believe you know about, from what Zeriel has told me."

"What do you seek with them?" he asked, watching my brief exchange with Hansa.

"Support. They're loyal to Sverik, and, now that he's out of Azazel's prison, they'll be willing to pledge their support and join our ranks. We need all the able bodies we can get," Draven replied.

"How do you know they're his bodyguards?" I whispered to Hansa.

"They're well-built and highly attentive. You see them quiet and motionless, but watch me make a move and see how they react. They see and hear everything and follow our every gesture. I was too fast, even for them." She grinned with satisfaction.

I had a feeling she'd really enjoyed showing Jax that she was faster than him. Not that I could blame her. Despite my initial dismay at Hansa potentially ruining our alliance with the Maras, I couldn't exactly fault her, but I wouldn't have done it.

"Now you're the one underestimating us, succubus," Jax interjected.

Hansa and I stilled, then looked at him. He leaned back in his chair, smirking as a young Mara female brought him a golden chalice. He sipped slowly, licking his lips.

"They're not bodyguards. They are wards," he added. "They follow me everywhere and ward off any spells or mental attacks aimed at me. They do not fight with their swords. They are very special creatures."

He snapped his fingers, and one of the Maras we were talking about took a few steps forward, standing next to Jax's chair. He was young and tall, with a broad frame and eyes the color of pine forests. He removed his cloak, revealing his bare chest and leather pants, as well as the myriad of black ink tattoos on his entire upper body. I gasped as I recognized the tattoos as symbols from the swamp witches' spell books.

"That's swamp witch magic," I exclaimed. "Where'd you get that?"

"All my wards have it. It's how the Lord of Maras is protected. We once helped a swamp witch, and she returned the favor. Unlike the Tritones, who have yet to repay their debt to us," Jax replied and gave Zeriel a reprimanding look.

The Tritone sighed and put his arms forward on the table, a look of defeat on his face.

"Fine, take it now. Just don't take too much and don't leave any marks. I hate doing this," he mumbled.

"What is he talking about?" I asked Jax.

"Pyrope. I saved Zeriel's life. I saved his entire family from a most slow and painful death once."

"But what's Pyrope?"

"It's a blood payment." Zeriel sighed.

A Mara approached him with a slim knife and another golden chalice in his hands. I wanted to say something, but I felt Draven's hand beneath the table, his fingers digging into my thigh and prompting me to stay still. I watched as the Mara cut Zeriel's arm and let the blood pour into the chalice for several minutes. Then, he licked his finger and dabbed it on the open wound. Zeriel's cut healed instantly, leaving a faint scar behind. The Mara delivered the goblet to Jax, who took it and gulped it down in an instant.

I stilled then, as the familiarity of the gesture brought back instant memories of home, The Shade...my family.

"Zeriel hasn't paid his debt in five months, but now the

balance is restored." Jax smiled and licked his lips. My jaw dropped as I watched his canines become sharper and longer as his tongue passed over them. Then the canines retreated slowly.

My heart stopped for a second. The similarities continued to crash into me. Zeriel had told us they didn't go out during the day. The drinking of blood. The fangs. The pale skin. The weird glow in their eyes and their mind-bending abilities were something new, but everything else pointed to the same species. Vampires. I had a feeling the Maras were somehow Eritopia's version of vampires—just like Eritopia had its own brand of witches.

"I've seen creatures like you before," I croaked, as Zeriel gulped down some water. "Well, somewhat like you. You do have a couple of differentiating features, but your species is very familiar to me."

Jax looked at me, his eyes small and lips pursed, waiting for me to continue.

"Back home, in my world, beyond the In-Between, they're called vampires." I leaned forward with bated breath. "Please, tell me more about your kind."

Jax frowned, examining my face for a long moment, before he began. "Well, there used to be more of us. Many more. But Azazel's forces caught us by surprise. Many were killed in their sleep or by his wretched spells. This city is one of the last few safe places in Eritopia, but even this won't last much longer. The swamp witch only managed to give the ward tattoos to the Maras you see in this hall before she was lured out of the city.

Unfortunately, we didn't know how to recreate the spell." Jax paused.

"What about the fangs? The blood?" I pressed, too interested in their physiology to care much about their history in this moment.

"It's how we feed. We drink red blood only. We try to limit ourselves to animals these days. Before Azazel, we used to find ourselves creatures outside our species to feed off whenever we needed. In return, we healed them and their loved ones when they needed it."

"Why just red blood? And do you only feed from other species, or do you also feed from other Maras?" My racing mind also couldn't help but wonder whether they'd ever tried feeding off incubi or succubi, since their blood was silver and unlike anything I'd ever seen before. I wondered if the Maras found it nourishing in any way, as the vampires I knew had never tasted anything other than red blood.

"Silver blood is highly toxic to us. Silver in general. There's something in the metal's composition that just doesn't work well for our immune system," he replied, his gaze fixed on Sverik, who'd broken into a cold sweat. "And no, we don't feed off each other. Our own blood doesn't provide us with any sustenance, which is why we feed off other creatures. Nowadays it's harder to find people willing to give us their blood, so we hunt animals from the woods nearby."

"And you don't like the sunlight, either," I said. "Aida's

brother saw Maras at the Sarang Marketplace a few days back in broad daylight. How does that work?"

"The sun burns. Overexposure will kill a Mara. We do have a spell left from the swamp witches to protect us over short periods of time. Whoever you saw at Sarang was probably using the spell. We generally stick to our night cycle, as the bones of a Deargh really aren't easy to come by these days."

The sun burns. Overexposure will kill. Just like our Shade vamps. They even relied on magic spells to protect themselves—probably the same fire protection spell we'd used to travel between volcanoes. It all felt so surreal.

"How does one become a Mara?" I asked, desperate to know more.

Jax gave me a confused look. "One does not *become* a Mara. One can only be born a Mara," he replied.

I stared, trying to process the information, then nodded slowly. In addition to the Maras' ability to influence minds, *this* was a crucial difference between them and our vampires. A part of me had started to worry there might be some kind of Elder-counterpart here in Eritopia, but no. The Maras were a species in their own right, and they must be able to reproduce just like any other creature.

"And the mind-bending? How does that work? How exactly do you influence minds?" I asked.

"We cannot read minds, like you tried to do earlier." He grinned at me, making me blush.

So he had sensed it. He just didn't show it.

"We bend wills, plant suggestions. Hypnosis and persuasion, mostly. We make creatures forget or believe whatever we want them to believe, including that they could fly if they threw themselves off a cliff, or that fire doesn't burn. Some of us have honed this skill to induce hallucinations."

"Mind tricks," I concluded, completely in awe of what he was telling me. As a sentry, I had the ability to read emotions and control minds, while the Maras basically seemed to be masters of hypnotic trickery. Nevertheless, I was unable to read a Mara's mind, which made me wonder whether Jax could use his powers on me. I considered the possibility of our mental abilities cancelling each other out.

"Call them what you wish. They have kept us alive for millennia," he replied. "Playing mind tricks on our invaders has become a solid trademark. But it won't hold them off forever, which is why I must admit I am pleased to see you all here tonight with your alliance offer."

"How is White City still safe?" I asked. My eyes wandered around the hall and noticed Sverik shifting uncomfortably in his chair. Hansa was busy peeling a bright orange fruit. Zeriel was still working his way through some grapes, while Draven watched the exchange between the Mara and me.

"The woods on the eastern side of this mountain are thick and dark. We have Maras stationed there all the time, taking turns mind-bending any curious creatures to go away. The last time we had Destroyers try to come in, we managed to plant illusions in their heads, enough to make them go back on their own, convinced that there was nothing beyond that forest for them to see. It was a close call, but I don't know how long we have left before Azazel descends upon us. There are enough of us here to instill fear in small numbers trying to invade, even Destroyers. Unfortunately, we've not been able to push them into killing each other. Illusions and hysterias have worked quite well. Should they come in much larger numbers, however, I don't think we'll be so lucky."

I nodded and looked around the table once more. Sverik seemed nervous. He bit into his fingernails while his gaze darted from one Mara to another. Jax shot him a cold glance and lifted an eyebrow. Hansa, Draven, and I exchanged a few glances, waiting quietly to hear a pledge of allegiance, like the Dearghs and Lamias before.

"It didn't seem real at first," he continued. "But seeing there are others out there resisting Azazel is what makes me want to join this fight. You have our word, our loyalty, and our strength, Druid."

A wave of relief washed over me, as I witnessed another species joining our war against Azazel. At the same time, I remembered the girls back at the mansion and my brother. They were still in danger, and we didn't know how the Destroyers would get past the protective shield.

"Thank you, Jax," Draven replied. "Your help is much needed and welcome. We've had a rough ride so far. Your strength will certainly help turn the tide in our favor again."

"The more of us there are, the higher our chance of success.

Having the Oracles on our side is certainly one of the aspects that persuades me to join you," Jax replied, then looked at Sverik persistently. "It's good to see there are still incubi who haven't succumbed to Azazel, either. I thought you were all gone."

Sverik shook his head, his mouth drawn into a thin line. "It wasn't easy," the incubus said. "I had to lose my brother to Destroyers to understand that my father made a mistake by aligning himself with Azazel. We'll get more help once we reach the incubi settlement. They'll be happy to stand up and fight with me, with us."

"Speaking of which, where is this settlement?" I asked Sverik.

"I will take you to it," Jax said before the incubus could reply. "They're well hidden, but they were never able to cloak themselves from us. We know everything that moves around this mountain and beyond the woods. I have a feeling Sverik hasn't seen this camp in a while and they know to not stay in one place for too long."

"Thank you," I replied. "When can we leave?"

"Within the hour, ideally. We're better off traveling at night around these parts."

Zeriel then stood up, beaming at us. He seemed to have recovered his strength. He stretched his arms outward.

"I will leave you with Jax, then, and be on my way," the Tritone said.

"Wait, why? I thought you were coming with us," I replied, confused.

Draven nudged me, enough to capture my attention. I noticed the disapproving look on his face and remembered Zeriel's advances and their effect on him. I mentally grinned.

"Have you not had enough of him already? Because I have," he muttered.

"Alas, I must go! I promised the Druid I'd rally more fighters for this alliance. I have a few doors to knock on," Zeriel replied, then grinned seductively my way, prompting another scowl from Draven. "Mind you, if you want me to stay, I can stay!"

"No, she's good," Draven shot back.

22

SERENA

T he Maras helped us replenish some of our dry food and water for the rest of our journey, and gave us some health potions in case of emergency. They'd brewed them with their own saliva, which I'd already noticed had healing properties. This was another stunning similarity to our vampires, whose blood could cure physical injuries. I made a mental note to ask Jax later about the extent of these healing properties.

Zeriel came to each of us for a farewell hug. He took an extra minute when he embraced me, holding me tight.

"I know your heart belongs to the Druid, Serena," the Tritone whispered in my ear. "But I just get a kick out of messing with him. I hope you can forgive me."

His confession made me laugh. He dropped a kiss on my forehead and rested his hands on my shoulders. I gave Draven a sideways glance and noticed his eyes flickering black and nostrils flaring. Zeriel was definitely hitting the spot with these gestures, but Draven had to keep himself calm and respectful; he couldn't risk fracturing an alliance over the meaningless advances of a Tritone. After all, had Zeriel been truly serious with these intentions, he would've been much more persistent, forcing Draven to eventually intervene.

"I'll leave you with the Maras now," Zeriel said, looking at both Draven and me. "And I shall see you on the night of the seventh moon at the northern waterfall of Mount Agrith. I will try to bring more creatures into the fold in the meantime, but I cannot promise anything."

"Thank you for trying, nonetheless," I said.

He nodded respectfully then slapped Jax on the shoulder in a half-friendly gesture.

"See you at the waterfall, Jax. Stay classy!"

Jax opened his mouth to say something, and, judging by the look on his face, it promised to be not at all friendly, but Zeriel chuckled and ran toward the beach, nearly flying down the stairs. The other Tritones bowed, then followed their young king into the water. I watched their colorful tails slap the water as they swam away.

"The impertinent fool," Jax muttered.

"You two seem to have quite the history," I replied.

"He is the closest thing I've had to a friend in a thousand years."

"And you forced him into a blood pact? That's cruel!"

"It's how we met, actually. His group had been caught in a

storm, stranded on our beach. He begged for my help, and I never grant anything for free. It is part of our ethos as Maras. So I asked for a sip of his blood at every full moon, for as long as he lives, in return for my help. He said yes, because it's in his nature to say yes without thinking much, and here we are. A thousand years later, and he is unchanged. We usually meet every month to catch up, but he's recently become King of the Tritones. I figured it's why he's been late for Pyrope, but he still has to pay the price," Jax explained.

It all made sense, though. Their friendship may have started out with a bargain, but it had made it to one thousand years. Jax didn't strike me as an instantly friendly guy. If anything, he came across as Zeriel's complete opposite. He seemed like the type who wouldn't open up to just anyone and who kept his guard up at all times. At the same time, he didn't mind sharing information when I asked him for it. Jax had taken an interest in me because I was a sentry. He seemed fine with telling me about himself and his kind, up to a point.

Jax and Zeriel had been around each other for a long time, and, despite the Mara's reserve and Zeriel's reluctance to fulfill his end of the bargain, neither seemed to mind. Pyrope sounded more like an excuse to meet than anything else. My mind wandered back to Aida and Vita for a second, as I hoped I'd live to get just as much time with them.

"I've known the Tritone for many years. Don't let his seemingly carefree demeanor fool you," Jax continued, watching Zeriel as he disappeared into the dark water. "Do not think him all giggles and smiles, Serena. The Tritones are jovial creatures, but they're also extremely territorial and do not take kindly to invaders. I've seen them rip others to shreds when they felt threatened. I'm sure you'll soon see them in action yourself."

It didn't occur to me to consider Zeriel as fierce and as ruthless as Jax described him. I had a hard time stepping away from the image of a bubbly Tritone who loved fooling around and hitting on me.

"I have to admit, I can't really picture Zeriel ripping anyone to shreds," I said. "But I reckon appearances can be deceiving."

"Of course appearances can be deceiving," Jax replied, glancing at Sverik, who noticed attention focused on him and frowned. "We all have hidden façades, little or giant secrets that nobody knows about. Why should Zeriel be any different?"

I sensed his absent tone, then looked at Sverik, who broke eye contact with Jax and scoffed, running a hand through his hair.

"Don't mess with my head, Mara!" he warned with a sharp voice.

"My apologies. Force of habit." Jax smirked. "I just wanted to make sure your intentions are honorable, since you seemed so nervous. Figured I could get you to tell me what was on your mind."

I realized then that the Lord of Maras had been consistently trying to play with Sverik's mind since the moment we'd arrived in the white marble hall. I remembered the incubus fidgeting and breathing heavily, looking around nervously and trying to keep his composure. Jax had watched him surreptitiously the whole time. He'd been using his mind-bending abilities on him, but I couldn't tell exactly how much. My first guess involved hallucinations or implanted thoughts, which Sverik, poor guy, had been resisting.

"We should get going soon," Jax said, then snapped his fingers.

Several Maras brought five horses to the base of the steps. Their hooves dug into the white sand. They were beautiful creatures, black pure bloods with midnight blue eyes and indigo manes.

"It will take us a couple of hours to reach the settlement," he added and got on one of the horses.

The animal responded to his presence, neighing and lifting itself on its hind legs. Jax patted its strong neck and clicked his tongue once, calming the steed. He looked at me and smiled.

"They respond wonderfully to a powerful mind. If they sense weakness, they will try to throw you off."

We took a less traveled path along the beach, moving north toward the incubi settlement. The moon shone brightly in a perfect night sky, casting its white light on the sand and glistening ocean water to our left.

Draven and I rode our horses right behind Jax, followed by Hansa and Sverik. We'd managed to keep our steeds under control, but Sverik's still neighed and stubbornly tried to trot away from the group.

Jax's fingers snapped and brought the animal back into submission each time.

"I told you, Sverik. They do not listen to weaklings," he quipped without bothering to look over his shoulder.

"I'm not a weakling! Your horse isn't too bright, that's all," Sverik snapped back.

I smiled, mostly to myself, remembering his screams when we passed through the stone and fell into the lagoon. I glanced over at Draven and found him looking at me. His gray eyes were dark and focused intensely on me.

"You were unbelievable today," he said quietly, a smile tugging at the corner of his mouth.

"I barely did anything," I replied, blushing.

I wasn't sure what he meant, but every time he acknowledged my contribution to this mission, my heart swelled with pride. I knew I was young and that there was still so much to learn, but I'd come a long way since I'd first arrived in Eritopia, and it felt good to see Draven point these things out.

"For a non-Eritopian, you really held it together from the moment we dropped through the passage stone. You're not afraid to speak to strangers who have the ability to kill you. To ask questions. To oppose something you feel is wrong. You have the makings of a leader, Serena. And it's an honor to have you with me."

His words touched something very deep inside of me as I

understood what he was saying. For a creature like him, raised in utter isolation, being able to bond and work through challenges the way he did with me must have been extraordinary.

"Thank you," I whispered and projected everything that I was feeling toward him.

His eyes grew wide, and I knew that he felt the wave of emotions that had been stirring up inside of me from the moment I'd first laid eyes on him. I wanted him to experience it all, and, judging by his softened gaze, I was content that I'd made myself clear.

"He's right, you know," Jax interjected nonchalantly. "For someone not from this world, you come across as an impressive creature. Now you've had your chance to drill me with questions about my kind; why don't you return the favor?"

"What would you like to know?" I asked, my voice dry. I sensed Draven's discomfort seeping through me. I knew he didn't like me getting all this attention, but it wasn't like we had much of a choice, given the circumstances. I gave him a gentle, reassuring smile and a wink and focused my attention on the Mara.

He was strange, mysterious, and had a very sharp tongue—similar to Draven from that perspective. But he'd been forthcoming about his species with me, so it seemed reasonable to repay the favor. After all, he had just put his neck on the line for us in this fight against Azazel.

"What is a sentry, Serena?" he asked. "I've never met your kind before."

"That's because we're not from around here. This isn't my world."

"That I understood from the very beginning. Tell me more."

"Have you ever heard of ghouls?" I asked, unsure whether they had such creatures in the In-Between.

"I've heard of them venturing into the In-Between on occasion but have never seen one personally," he replied.

"Well, ghouls are generally evil, vile creatures with the ability to control minds and implant visions into people's heads." I briefly explained how there had been a settlement of ghouls in Nevertide and how humans had contracted their nature—which eventually led to my parents meeting and me being conceived. "So, I'm basically part human, part ghoul," I concluded.

"Human," Jax murmured.

"Yeah. Though most of my family are vampires. We are the Novaks, a powerful vampire clan that has brought much balance and peace between different worlds and species. One day, I will also be given the choice to become a vampire or remain pure sentry," I said.

I noticed Draven's expression as he listened to my origin story. I realized I'd told him very little about where I was from, and yet I was sharing my life's story with a complete stranger. I couldn't help but feel a little guilty, although we hadn't had much time to spend talking about me. I still had so many questions about him left unanswered as well.

I decided to elaborate further. "Sentries evolved throughout the years into their own standalone species. They can turn other humans into sentries through...uh, intimate contact." I cleared my throat and reached into my satchel for a sip of water, then continued. "They can also be born, like me. We have a few abilities, some stronger than others, varying from one sentry to another. I can absorb the life force, the energy, out of other creatures. I need it every few days, otherwise I grow weak. I can read minds, or more particularly, emotions. I catch glimpses of images and thoughts, but I'm still learning to interpret everything. It doesn't work with everyone, like you pointed out earlier. I have something called True Sight, which means I can see for vast distances, even through objects. And I can hold my own in a fight."

I wasn't sure whether I should tell him about my barrier building abilities, mainly because I was still in the process of developing them and didn't want him to think me weak in any way. The one thing I'd learned in Eritopia was that those considered weak were vulnerable and the first to perish. I had to maintain myself above the line and not give anyone reason to try something against me.

While Jax may have joined our alliance, I wasn't sure he could be trusted fully, so I decided to keep some information to myself, just like we had kept the existence of the Daughter out of the conversation.

"You are quite fascinating, as I suspected," Jax said and pulled his horse back to trot alongside mine. "A lot like me, but something else entirely."

He gazed at me for a while, his expression firm. I noticed Draven's eyes flickering black as he looked ahead, most likely pretending to watch the road. Not that I didn't mind setting him on fire like this once in a while, but he'd already had a hard day with Zeriel's constant advances. I wasn't sure he needed another round of putting up with Jax's attention toward me—as innocent as it was, since this was just about the discovery of a similar species. I found the jealousy cute, though. It was reaffirming that whatever he felt for me, it was as deep as what I experienced every time I looked at him.

"I'm surprised to find a species so similar to the vampires back home. I think you and our kind would get along really well. I know my family would love to understand the Maras better, especially since you're all born into it. In our case, it's a disease that gives us incredible strength, reflexes, and eternal life but forces us out of the sunlight and into drinking blood for sustenance," I replied.

"I understand. You strike me as a very interesting creature, sentry. I would like to see you in action sometime, since you said you can hold your own in a fight. Since I've never met someone like you, I'm sure you understand my curiosity and willingness to put your skills to the test."

I scoffed, remembering the last time I'd been in a fight with Destroyers trying to rip me to shreds and poisoned spears whizzing past my head as I jumped into the river. I shook my head.

"Just because I said I can fight doesn't mean that I like it," I replied.

"You don't have to like it to be good at it. Some of us are simply born...great," he said, then clicked his tongue, making his horse go back to the front of our group.

23

SERENA

W e spent the next hour discussing details of our alliance and the roles that each of us would play, provided those we reached out to would join us. I learned a few more interesting details about the Maras as well, further cementing my belief that I'd come across Eritopian vampires. I thought about my parents and grandparents as our horses carried us through the thick woods north of White City, and whether I would even get to see them again to tell them about the discovery.

The existence of the Maras would certainly arouse their interest. Perhaps GASP would even consider studying them, collecting blood samples, and uncovering any other similarities between them and the vampires of The Shade.

"I heard about the Red Tribe massacre," Sverik said to

Hansa as they were riding behind us. I glanced over my shoulder to get a better look at both. "I am sorry for your loss."

Hansa took a deep breath, her gaze meeting mine for a second. "Thank you, Sverik. We will survive. We will rebuild. We will not be defeated. As long as Anjani and I are still alive, the Red Tribe will continue to exist," she replied.

"I have to say, I admire your strength," he said.

"We are succubi. We have no other choice, son of Arid."

Sverik scoffed, looking away with a pained expression. "Don't mention his name. I am where I am because of him, because of the way he raised me. I couldn't stand up to him, and when I finally gathered the courage to say something, Azazel laughed in my face and had me thrown in a cage to sit with the rest of his prisoners, while my father watched and did nothing."

Jax's horse slowed down, giving Draven and me the lead. The Mara moved closer to Sverik and Hansa as he watched the exchange between them with quiet interest.

"You are nothing like Kristos, you know," Hansa replied.

"Yes, Kristos was the star of the family. All my father's hopes were with him, that he would lead our clan to glory. When news of his death broke, we were shattered. It led to poor decisions, and we ended up serving Azazel," Sverik said, then looked at her. "You knew my brother?"

"A long time ago, yes. He was just a little boy when our paths crossed. The world is worse off without him now. Kristos had this awe-inspiring attitude, seemingly fearless and incredibly determined since he was but a child. I heard that he led successful campaigns against the Destroyers when they came for the Eastern Citadel."

"All the incubi and brilliant tactics at our disposal were not enough to keep Azazel's dark magic at bay, though," Sverik said. "He helped the city resist a few months longer than the others, but he was ultimately driven out by his own people. Their minds were tainted by Azazel. He was branded a deserter by the new power, and he joined the resistance, alongside Bijarki and the incubi we're going to meet later. They were forced to separate at some point, as Kristos and Bijarki headed south. It was the last time I heard anything about my brother before I was told he was dead. Afterward, the incubi they'd aligned themselves within the resistance were gone, vanished, impossible to trace. I know Azazel wanted them found and killed, but they never were."

A moment passed before Hansa spoke again.

"Kristos had the potential to become a great leader," she said.

I noticed how she and Jax looked at each other, never at the same time and only when the other wasn't looking. Jax occasionally fixed his gaze on her before shifting it back to Sverik, who was still visibly uncomfortable with the Mara's attention.

"Yes, well, he's gone now, and our clan is left with my foolish father and me, the loudmouth who never really liked war," the incubus said, a tinge of sadness in his voice.

Draven changed the subject. "Tell us about the incubi settlement. Have you met any of them personally?"

Sverik nodded. "Most of them were in my brother's garrison. They're grunts and scouts, expert marksmen, and ruthless in battle. They move freely across the plains and through the jungles as they've been part of the resistance for decades now, and they can spread the word to the right people regarding our alliance. They can bring valuable numbers into the fold, but we will have to earn their trust. After they were separated from Kristos and Bijarki, they kept a very low profile, so I'm not sure whom they've spoken to since."

"How do you know where the settlement is, then?" Draven replied.

"I still have contacts among the rogues. It wasn't easy, but I pinpointed their location shortly before I was imprisoned. I was going to tell my father about them, as I had been ordered, but once they threw me in a cage, I decided to keep it to myself."

"How noble of you, son of Arid," Jax interjected, his tone laced with sarcasm. It was becoming obvious that the Mara didn't like Sverik much.

"Wow, you really need to tone it down a little," the incubus shot back. "What did I ever do to you?"

"I just don't like weaklings, incubus. Let's not forget you did Azazel's bidding for a while."

"And I paid a hefty price when I was thrown in a cage!"

"Cut it out," Hansa barked at them, visibly annoyed. "We're in this together now, and Sverik is one of our own. Give him a break. He's been through enough as it is. I'm sure it couldn't have been easy for him, stuck between his father and brother."

"Hold on. Why are you making it sound like I'm traumatized and weak?" Sverik looked insulted. His eyes darted from Hansa to Jax.

"She doesn't need to make it sound like you're weak," the Mara replied. "It's already obvious."

Sverik scoffed and kicked his horse in an attempt to put some distance between him and Jax, but the animal was once again unwilling to cooperate, neighing and lifting itself on its hind legs before it trotted away into the woods.

"No, don't!" Sverik shouted at his horse to no avail. "What are you doing? No!"

I couldn't help but chuckle, watching as the incubus was carried into the forest by a very stubborn horse. I looked at Jax, who looked vaguely amused. Hansa shook her head slowly.

"Did you do something to his horse?" I asked Jax.

"Absolutely nothing. I told you these are special creatures. They sense weakness and do not obey unless they're shown strength and determination."

"Then fix it!" Hansa snapped, pointing in Sverik's direction. "Get him back!"

Jax exhaled sharply and patted his horse on the neck. It trotted after Sverik. I heard neighing and hooves rumbling in the darkness. A minute later, the Mara and Sverik emerged from the woods and rejoined the group. Jax was trying to stifle a smirk, while the incubus was sullen and glowing with embarrassment.

"By the Daughters, I'm stuck with a Druid, a sentry, and two children," Hansa grumbled and moved in front of the group.

Jax put on a straight face and joined her. His jade eyes settled on her profile as she kept riding and avoided his gaze. I had a feeling he was interested in her, but I wasn't sure what that interest entailed. It was difficult to read him based solely on his facial expressions.

Draven and I looked at each other, projecting our emotions in warm waves of gold and pink. Words of affection were risky outside of the mansion's protective shield, and we both knew it. We were in foreign territory, in the company of others, and about to meet potentially hostile incubi. After all, aside from their location and what they'd once done with Kristos and Bijarki, we knew nothing else about them.

Some years had passed, and there was a chance that they may not be interested in an alliance anymore. They might be focused solely on surviving, or worse, just hopeless and waiting to die.

Whatever came next, one thing I knew for sure; I looked forward to another moment alone with Draven. There were still many words left unspoken between us to describe how we felt about each other. With each moment, I became more and more aware that whatever was going on between us was growing. It was increasing in intensity until it was difficult to imagine a future without him.

Another hour passed before we saw lights flickering in the distance, scattered across the beach and into the neighboring woods. The incubi settlement was barely a hundred yards away as we left the woods behind us.

"We're here," Jax said.

Sverik rode forward until he reached Jax's side to get a better look. He glanced at us over his shoulder and smiled with newfound confidence.

"Let me do the talking," he said. "They're more likely to speak to an incubus."

The four of us watched him as he went ahead. I used my True Sight. The incubi had sensed movement and could see us approaching. They rushed for their weapons, pulling knives and swords out of their sheaths and taking their defensive stances.

I tried to warn him. "Sverik, I don't think it's a good idea."

The sound of feet shuffling through the sand caught my attention.

Several dark figures approached us from all angles, obscured by the darkness as the moon hid behind a cloud. My True Sight quickly revealed them as incubi holding knives and baring their teeth.

The settlement was now fifty feet away, and it was riddled with rogues readying themselves for a fight. Some had already taken the initiative to give us a not-so-friendly greeting.

"Don't move," Jax ordered.

His eyes lit up, and his arms reached out to both sides, fingers spread wide.

24

JOVI

L ater in the day, the succubi were waiting downstairs in the banquet hall, filling up on a hearty lunch. I came in last, finding Phoenix, the Daughter, and Anjani already at the table, sipping coffee and talking about the Destroyers waiting outside. I'd seen Bijarki go into the upstairs study room, most likely to look over the maps of Calliope to plan out the campaign against Azazel.

I sat down next to Anjani and poured myself a mug as I glanced at her. She hadn't slept much the night before. I could tell from her tired eyes and slow movements. I'd barely caught an hour of sleep myself. I'd spent the night alone in my bed, hoping I'd hear her knock on my door. We'd gotten so close during our stay at the River Pyros that I'd expected her to want to spend her nights with me.

I figured she must have spent the night with her sisters,

catching up after the Red Tribe tragedy, so I didn't go looking for her. I gave her space in the morning as well, as she looked after her sisters and served breakfast.

The Oracles had gone through another session of visions, with Field watching over them.

"Didn't sleep much?" I asked Anjani. I filled my plate with food.

She shook her head and smiled.

"Barely an hour or two. I stayed with my sisters until we all fell asleep. You don't look so well either." She raised an eyebrow at me.

"I find I sleep a lot better with you in my arms," I replied, my voice low.

I watched her expression change into something soft and sweet, glowing momentarily before she looked away, focusing on her sisters. I'd made her blush. One more point for Jovi.

"They are safe here," she said. "I'm so relieved to see them."

"I know what you mean," I told her. "I don't know what I would do if anything happened to Aida."

I didn't see Aida in the hall, and Field and Vita were also missing.

"Have you seen her since your vision session?" I asked Phoenix.

His mouth was full of steamed vegetables. He shook his head and pointed his fork upward. He swallowed. "Aida and Vita are sleeping upstairs. We had a rough one. Field's outside working out," he said.

"Okay, well, share anything you can with us when you're ready. What about the Lamias?"

"I have no idea, and, frankly, I'm not too keen on finding out either. They're in here somewhere, as insufferable as ever. I offered them dinner last night, and they just scoffed and walked away."

"They're not the easiest to be around, especially since we're all confined to this mansion. As big as it is, it still feels small when you don't like the company," Anjani chimed in.

"Speaking of which," Olia said, pouring herself another coffee, "the girls and I spoke earlier, while you were showering. We're not going to stay here."

Anjani stilled halfway through a mouthful, her gaze fixed on Olia.

"What do you mean?" she replied.

"We're of no use to anyone here, Anjani. We need to be out there, rallying more troops against Azazel. Assuming Hansa made it safely through the passage stone, she's out there reaching out to other creatures. We can't stay here and just wait. We should be doing the same in the southwestern region. There are plenty of rogues in that area who would be thrilled to join our alliance," Olia explained.

"No. Absolutely not." Anjani shook her head. "You barely escaped death. You need to stay put. You're protected here!"

"For how long will we be protected?" Perra intervened. "According to the Oracles, the Destroyers will get in at some point. We don't need to be protected. We need to be out there fulfilling our duties, supporting this alliance. We need more soldiers, and you know it."

"No! You cannot leave! There are Destroyers just waiting for any one of us to come out. You won't make it fifty feet in any direction!"

"There's the invisibility spell," the Daughter chimed in.

"The what now?" Olia's focus shifted to the Daughter's face.

"No! Draven took some of it and left us with the rest in case something went wrong here with the shield. There isn't enough, and you know it will take months to regrow the ingredients needed for it," Anjani replied, then looked at Olia. "Forget about it!"

"There's enough to last about a mile for a small group of people," the Daughter said. "It will be enough to keep them cloaked for long enough to get out of the Destroyers' range."

"You're not helping." Anjani sighed.

"Your sisters do have a point," I said to her, realizing that she'd been trying to withhold the invisibility spell from the succubi to prevent them from leaving.

She gave me a death glare, and I instantly raised my hands in a defensive gesture. I knew she was only being protective of her sisters, but she had to accept the practical side of things. We needed help from wherever we could get it.

"Just hear me out, Anjani," I pleaded. "I can't go out, and neither can the Daughter or Field or any of the Oracles. Neither can Bijarki, who's got a bounty on his head. We're at high risk out there right now, and Azazel will sense the Oracles if they leave the shield. You need to stay here and protect them and the Daughter. You've sworn an oath to your sister, remember?"

A few seconds passed before she nodded, pursing her lips. She didn't like where this was going, clearly, but she was beginning to see the bigger picture as she looked at her sisters.

"The succubi, on the other hand, are more inconspicuous," I added. "And if they use the invisibility spell, they can get out of here with a higher chance of success. They're fast, and they know the jungles. They know where to go and whom to look for regarding our alliance. And there are plenty of them to protect each other. I am sorry, but your sisters are of more use out there than in here."

"Besides, we're big girls. We can take care of ourselves. You shouldn't underestimate us like this," Olia reprimanded her.

"I just don't like the idea of you out there and me stuck in here, unable to reach you," Anjani muttered, leaning against the back of her chair.

"I don't think that's a problem anymore," the Daughter replied.

"What do you mean?" Anjani asked.

"Phoenix and I were up most of the night translating more spells from the swamp witches' book. I found a spell that will help you keep in touch with your sisters," she explained.

"It sounds like a telepathy spell, from what I understood," Phoenix added. "It's a shame it didn't come up sooner, before Serena left through the passage stone, but the Daughter has yet to regain full control of Eritopia's cryptic languages. It takes her a while to translate some spells. We can at least try and use it with your sisters."

The succubi looked at each other, smiles stretching over their faces as Anjani rolled her eyes and nodded her consent.

"Fine! I won't stop you!" Anjani said, then glanced at the Daughter. "What do you need for the spell? How does it work?"

"We need the blood of all those you wish to reach out to, a few drops from each, and yourself," the Daughter replied. "Once they are out of here, you can perform the spell yourself to communicate with them. The book calls it a connection of spirits. I don't know exactly how it works. I only know how to prepare and perform it."

"We'll get ready, then!" Olia beamed from across the table.

An hour later, we gathered outside the mansion. Phoenix and the Daughter had collected the succubi's silver blood in small glass vials, placing them in a small wooden box, along with a scroll and several small bottles filled with colorful powders, which they handed to Anjani.

"This is the spell?" she asked, carefully analyzing the ingredients in the box.

The Daughter nodded. "Whenever you want to reach out to your sisters, follow the scroll's instructions. "It will help you communicate with them."

"You will be able to talk to each other in real time," Phoenix added.

The succubi had dressed in their leather garments. Their travel satchels were tied on their backs, and their swords hung loosely from their belts. The younger teens were by Anjani's side, as she had insisted that the girls stay behind.

They hugged and bid their farewells, whispering words of comfort and confidence to each other. I watched Anjani swallow back tears as she gave her sisters advice on where to go and how to travel the long distances that they needed to travel.

"Thank you for understanding." Olia wrapped her arms around Anjani. "I will see you soon. I promise!"

"You had better! We need to restore the glory of our Red Tribe, and I can't do it on my own!" she replied.

"We'd best be leaving now to get the most of the daylight. There are several camps east of Sarang Marketplace. We'll head there first," Perra said.

Phoenix passed the bowl with the prepared invisibility spell. The succubi took a handful each, which they ingested and washed down with some water.

"Now recite the spell as I've shown you," he said.

The succubi cleared their throats and straightened their backs, solemnly repeating the swamp witches' invisibility spell.

"In darkness and light, we will not be seen. Shapeless creatures we shall become, foreign to the eyes of anything that moves. Between leaves and against stones, through water and dirt, we shall be like air. Unseen, obscured, concealed. We shall be cloaked in light, reflecting light, exuding light."

They looked at each other, then at Phoenix and the Daughter.

"So, what now?" Olia asked. "We disappear?"

"Exactly," Phoenix said and nodded toward the sisters.

Olia gasped as she watched the succubi around her glimmer and vanish gradually. The spell had worked perfectly.

"This will hold you for about a mile, based on Serena and Draven's previous experience with it," Phoenix added.

"Good. We're leaving now." I heard Olia's voice in the spot where she'd last been visible.

"Please, be careful," Anjani said. She waved goodbye.

She took a deep breath as we heard their steps through the grass. They reached the protective shield, where several Destroyers were patrolling, absently looking around. The barrier shimmered lightly. It was barely noticeable—the Destroyers weren't aware that the succubi were slipping through their fingers.

I looked at Anjani and noticed the pained look in her emerald-gold eyes, glazed with tears. I moved closer and wrapped an arm around her shoulders. She caved in, sobbing as she hid her face in my chest, her hands settling on my sides. I held her as she shuddered.

Phoenix and the Daughter took the young succubi back inside the mansion. The girls glanced over their shoulders, visibly concerned about Anjani, but I heard Phoenix reassure them that she would be okay.

I smiled, thankful to have him as a friend. A reliable fighter who had almost died trying to protect me was capable of babysitting two teenage succubi, even if they could barely sit still for more than five minutes.

"It'll be okay," I said to Anjani, my body filled with the familiar warmth of her touch.

She took deep breaths, relaxing in my embrace.

"Thank you," she whispered and looked at me.

"For what?"

"For...you."

Anjani had this way of flooring me with just a handful of words. I ran my fingers through her curly black hair, then traced an invisible line along her jaw before I touched her lower lip.

"I could say the same thing," I replied and dropped a gentle peck on the tip of her nose.

She blinked several times, then pushed herself up on the tips of her toes to kiss me. I welcomed her warm sweetness. Our lips parted and molded in perfect union. It felt so right, even with death waiting for us beyond the shield.

The wolf's head pendant seemed heavier in my pocket as I deepened the kiss, caressing her face and breathing in her scent.

Who was I fooling? I couldn't possibly see myself giving that pendant to anyone else. It made no sense to look any further for a soulmate. I'd already found her.

The Daughter and I left the young succubi girls in the greenhouse, which seemed like their favorite part of the mansion. They used some of the gardening tools stored in a box there to trim the potted trees and collect various flowers for poisons, saying they wanted to make sure that their big sister had everything she needed in case of an attack.

I found their support and devotion heartwarming, as I understood that the succubi were taught from a very young age to love and protect each other. It only made the Red Tribe massacre an even greater tragedy. I understood Anjani's reluctance to let her other sisters go, but they served a better purpose out there than stuck in the mansion with us.

The Daughter and I made our way to my room, where she lay down. She was determined to reach out to her sisters after our conversation in Draven's study. It had taken her a while to calm down after she'd heard about her fate and ours and the explosion. In fact, keeping her mind busy with preparing the spells for the succubi had worked, but as Anjani's sisters vanished, I could feel her slipping away and desperation taking hold of her once again.

"I need to speak to them," the Daughter mumbled.

I lay in bed next to her. I dropped a kiss on her forehead and watched as her eyes closed. She drifted away. My soul was connected to hers even as she slept. I felt everything that went on inside of her, every moment of angst and every sliver of fear. I also sensed the warmth she exuded from her core each time I got close to her. Emotions poured out of her and filled me up with liquid sunshine. Most importantly, I felt the energy stored inside of her, the source of the future devastating explosion described by Vita. It shook me, sending shivers down my spine and leaving me in awe of what she was capable of.

Yet, she didn't want to hurt anyone. She didn't want the pain, the suffering, the uncertainty that we dealt with daily.

Her breathing became heavy, and I felt a pang in my stomach. Something was wrong. She was experiencing something very dark and painful, and I could sense it. She frowned and whimpered, moving her head.

I kissed her temple in an attempt to soothe her, but she continued to get more restless in her sleep.

Her eyes flew open and glowed violet. She sat up and gasped for air. She blinked several times before she looked at me, fear imprinted on her beautiful face. Beads of sweat glistened on her skin, and she brought her hand up to touch my lips with trembling fingers.

"I saw my sisters," she said. Tears rolled down her cheeks. "They waited for me in the darkness. They wore their gold masks and silk garments. Their fingers were covered in rings and gemstones. They stood there, looking at me, telling me that I had to sacrifice myself in order to save Eritopia."

She sobbed, and I took her in my arms.

"I asked them if there was another way. I told them that I didn't want to hurt you or anyone else. I asked them if there was another way to save you. To save us all. And they shook their heads! They just shook their heads, saying that my sacrifice was needed. And then I asked them about the other Daughter, the one Azazel has."

"What did they say?" I asked.

"They said she was their mistake, that Azazel snatched her egg a long time ago when it first emerged on Mount Agrith. Her egg was the first sign that Eritopia was in trouble as he expanded his dark reign, and they ignored her. They considered her to be a glitch, because they were everything that Eritopia needed against anyone and anything, including Azazel.

"They said the Destroyer was cunning and didn't pass on the opportunity to gain leverage against the Daughters, so he stole her egg and forced the Daughter inside to hatch prematurely. You see, the Daughters mature inside the eggs, and if we're hatched before our time, our growth stops, which is why he refers to her as 'the little one'. We cannot mature outside the egg. She's barely a girl and most likely has less of a clue about her abilities than I do. I spent more time in my egg, making me older than her, even though her egg came out first... Nevertheless, there is great power inside her and she is crucial to Eritopia's balance, making her extremely important. They said she is the only reason they haven't been able to wipe him out of existence. He's found a way to draw the energy he needs for his dark magic from her, not just the volcanoes. It's how he's built up such a resistance to everything. The Daughters cannot save our little sister, but Azazel has to be stopped. They said I'm the only way, that it must be why Mount Agrith pushed my egg to the surface shortly after she was taken."

I took a deep breath and ran my fingers through her hair, carefully considering everything she'd just told me.

"At least now we know why they never intervened and why they've resorted to adjacent measures to contain Azazel. He's drawing power from a Daughter he's holding hostage," I concluded, resting my head on top of hers.

She looked at me, her hands cupping my face as she swallowed back more tears.

"They are afraid to lose her, and they keep telling me to sacrifice myself to destroy Azazel," she said, her whole body shaking. "Why is her life more important than mine?"

I felt anger pouring out of her, along with red ribbons of pain, which I captured and absorbed in an attempt to make her feel better. I shook my head, my gaze locked on hers.

"I don't know, but I know one thing for sure. They do not

deserve you. And if they won't help you, we'll find another way. We'll put our minds together. We'll look at all possible options, and we'll find a better way to destroy Azazel."

She listened to me, clinging to every word as her fingers started digging into my shoulders. I felt her desperation, her eagerness to hope, to look elsewhere, to find an alternative to Vita's vision. My heart peeled itself open, layer after layer, and I understood how much she wanted to be here with me. It hadn't been so accurate, so perfectly clear before. I had sensed it but not with such intensity.

"We're connected," I added. "My heart to yours. My life to yours. I have no intention of finding out what happens if one of us dies. Do you understand me?"

Her eyes glimmered gently. The frown faded, the skin on her forehead smoothed over, and her lips stretched into a hopeful smile.

"We will live," she said.

I kissed her.

She leaned into me.

I wrapped my arms around her waist and pulled her even closer. My pulse raced as she opened up to me, and I felt the warmth of her feelings pouring through my veins.

Our connection was so strong and intimate, it made my heart pound against my ribcage. I couldn't get enough of her, of everything she had to give. Everything we experienced was of cosmic intensity, and my body reacted in equal measure to hers.

I deepened the kiss. My fingers traced her waist through the gentle fabric of her dress. She quivered and pushed her chest forward, pressing herself against me and nearly making me lose my mind.

I lifted my head to look at her in all her splendor—lips pink and tender, parted and yearning for more, eyes electrifyingly violet, and breath ragged. I felt excitement and intense curiosity seeping through her consciousness, as she ran her hands up and down my back, touching every muscle.

"I'm not leaving your side, you beautiful creature," I whispered and took her in my arms again, willing myself back into control.

She relaxed in my embrace, exhaling and purging the last wisps of darkness from her emotions as she found comfort in my presence. I held her close on the bed, listening to her breathing.

"Maybe next time you speak to your sisters, they can tell you your name." I smiled, my lips pressed on her forehead. "I don't know what to call you."

"I don't ever want to see them or speak to them again," she muttered, then looked at me. "Why don't you give me a name, instead?"

I took a deep breath, getting another whiff of her lilies and summer-at-the-beach scent. I was once again stunned by the way she rattled my every sense. I was hopeless, lifeless without her.

"Okay then, we'll find you a name. I'll think about it. You think about it too. We'll pick one together."

"Perfect," she murmured and nestled her face in my chest.

We were in a heap of trouble, since the Daughters had proven to be so unreliable. In fact, I'd lost a substantial amount of respect for them upon hearing they'd been so careless. They'd left a window open for Azazel to snatch their sister. They were exceptionally powerful but helpless, since the Destroyer held one of them hostage, feeding off her and gaining enough strength to resist them. Vita's vision made more sense. The Daughter tried to kill him with her touch, but it didn't work.

And yet, with one sister taken, they were adamant that the other would have to sacrifice herself to destroy Azazel, because they couldn't do anything else aside from their masked interventions. The advice they'd given Draven before blinding him, the visions they'd sent me, the diamond they'd given to the succubi during their prayer, the shroud that they'd placed on the whole of Eritopia to keep Azazel in and everyone else out; all were signs that they wanted to get involved but couldn't do much.

It was unfair but not impossible to work with. Just like they'd found other ways to help the world that birthed them, I would find a better way to defeat Azazel without the Daughter's sacrifice. I couldn't live without her, and I couldn't bear the thought of her suffering, even for a minute, because of her sisters' negligence. We would figure something out.

Anjani and I held each other for a while before I heard a long, torturous sigh leave her body. I was working up my courage to present her with the pendant. I'd made my decision, but I wasn't sure what her reaction would be.

"What's wrong?" I asked, my fingers fiddling with one of her curls.

"I can't help it. I'm just worried about the girls. I don't know if they made it out okay."

"Hmm." I nodded. "Why don't we try the spell then? Never too early, I say."

She looked up and gave me a broad smile.

I realized I was procrastinating, but I took her to Draven's study without saying a word about my feelings. She sat on the floor, opened the spell scroll, and prepared the ingredients. She dripped Olia's blood from one of the vials onto the symbol that the Daughter had drawn on the parchment. She looked up, her emerald-gold eyes twinkling as her gaze found mine. She then resumed the telepathy spell ritual, pouring dust from each little bottle over the blood and following the same pattern on the floor.

"They're a few hundred feet away by now, maybe more," she said.

I couldn't help but smile, amused by her curiosity and eagerness to speak to her sisters. I would've done the same if Aida were out like that, so I sat down next to her, watching quietly as she finished preparing the spell.

"Okay, now I have to read the incantation and set this thing on fire," she said, lifting the scroll from the floor to read it. "Our bodies, our souls, our minds, and our hearts connected. Be there land or water between us, I will hear you. Be there fire or ice between us, you will hear me. Open yourself to me, Olia. Let me in."

She then lit a match and set the symbol on fire. The powders burned in a dizzying array of reds and yellows as they fused with Olia's blood. The flames went out, leaving behind the symbol drawn in a fine black line.

Anjani inhaled sharply, her eyes rolling in her head. I froze, not sure what was happening and if the spell was working. She gasped, then smiled. Her eyes stayed white.

"Olia," she said. "I can...I can hear you!"

She laughed lightly, clapping her hands with joy as she stared blankly ahead.

"Yes," she answered.

I couldn't hear anything, but Anjani was definitely in touch with Olia. The spell had worked perfectly. "Yes, I understand. Where are you now?"

I kept quiet, gazing at her as she spoke to her sister, my heart filling itself up with all the emotions that had been crashing into me from the moment I'd first met her. I couldn't seem to get enough of her.

"Right, so you all made it out? Perfect! No, you want to keep heading southeast, and stay in the jungles along the roads... Yes, they might still be there... I suggest you wait another day if you have to. Just don't approach them at night. You don't want to catch them hungry. Let them hunt first..."

I shifted from a sitting position to my knees, resting on my calves as I dug into my pocket for the pendant. I felt unable to take my eyes off her. The smile she wore was as brilliant as a full moon. Her ink black hair covered her shoulders in a cascade of rich curls, and her skin gently shimmered.

"I will reach out to you again tomorrow evening, Olia. Please look after yourself and keep our sisters out of trouble, too. You're the eldest there. The responsibility falls on you." She chuckled, then stilled. "I love you too, sister."

Her eyes closed for a moment. She sighed as she recovered from the spell. She looked around, irises back to normal. Her gaze settled on me once more. She beamed with joy and bit into her lower lip, setting all kinds of fires inside me.

"It worked," she whispered. "I can check in on them once in a while. Those swamp witches were truly extraordinary."

"Indeed they were, Anjani," I said, trying to find the right moment to tell her how I felt. "I need to—"

"It's a shame we didn't discover this spell sooner!" she exclaimed, still in awe of her connection with Olia.

"Well, now we have it and can use it every time we get separated. Anjani, I—"

"I am amazed. Can you believe it? I can't believe it! Also, it's the first time I've done a spell all on my own," Anjani went on. "I mean, sure, the Daughter and Phoenix drew the blood and prepared the powders, but still, I was perfectly capable of following instructions and performing the entire spell!"

I took a deep breath, not sure whether she'd finished her ecstatic monologue or not. My palms sweated in my pockets while my heart galloped faster with each second that passed. I struggled to find the right words to express myself.

"The swamp witches were unbelievable. It's such a shame they're gone now, but they've left a tremendous legacy behind. Who else can summon magic with carefully compiled combinations of symbols, ingredients, and words, hm? No one! Not even the Druids!" she said.

"I'm in love with you." I held my breath.

Her eyes opened wide, and her lips parted, speechless.

"What... What?" she whispered.

I inhaled deeply. Saying it again took the same toll on me. I had a feeling it wasn't going to get any easier. My voice trembled, and my heart got stuck in my throat.

"I'm in love with you, Anjani."

A moment passed. She blinked several times, not taking her eyes off me.

"I know, you must think I'm crazy. I probably am. But since Vita's visions of my possible death, I've taken the value of my time alive more seriously. I don't want to waste another second, and I don't want any more time to pass without me telling you how I feel. I'm in love with you."

She didn't say anything. I'd obviously shocked her. The intensity of what I felt toward her scared me, but it had to be said. My stomach was a jumble of tight knots as I looked deep into her eyes, trying to identify something, anything, that would point to what she was feeling.

"I think I fell for you from the moment I first saw in the swamp waters. I knew there was no way I was letting those shifters harm you. I am crazy. I am crazy by nature, and I am crazy about you, Anjani. Your wit, your spirit, your determination, and your scent, the way you melt in my arms whenever I hold you, the way you respond to my kisses, the taste you leave in my mouth. It's all so inexplicably you and so incredible, I can't get enough of you, Anjani. You give me strength. You make me look forward to every single day. You're the first thing on my mind when I wake up and the last thought I have before I fall asleep. So I'll say it again. I love you."

My fingers felt the wolf's head pendant, tracing its shape in my pocket. Her silence was starting to make me nervous. I'd bared my soul, and I needed a response from her. At this point, anything worked, as long as she said something. As long as she acknowledged everything I'd just told her.

"Please say something," I mumbled, barely hearing myself.

"What do you want me to say, Jovi?" she replied, her husky voice turning me into a tinderbox ready to burst into flames.

"Anything."

"I don't like it when you talk about death. About you dying. That's not going to happen. It's why Vita has these visions—for us to prevent them from coming true," she said.

Her reply wasn't what I'd expected. My pulse continued to race from anxiety. I took the pendant out of my pocket, holding it by its delicate silver chain. The crystal between the wolf's teeth glistened under the candlelight, as it dangled before her. Her eyes grew even wider.

"What is that?"

"I got it from an old fae at the marketplace," I croaked. "She told me to only give it to my soulmate. So, here I am, giving it to you. I don't know whether you feel what I feel with the same intensity, but...I would like you to have this, no matter what."

A minute went by. The pendant dangled on its chain from my fingers, while her eyes followed its swaying movements, as if hypnotized. She lifted a hand and took it. She stared at it for a while, analyzing each line and facet carefully before she looked at me again, her eyes glazed with tears.

"Jovi, I...I'm a warrior," she breathed. "I was raised to never rely on a male, to never let myself feel anything other than love and devotion toward my sisters and my tribe. You are an anomaly."

It was my turn to blink, confused by the word she'd chosen to describe me.

She didn't give me a chance to respond. She closed the distance between us and kissed me. I felt like I was collapsing on the inside and gladly took everything she had to give me.

"I'm hopelessly in love with you, Jovi," she mumbled against my lips. "It goes against everything I've been taught as a succubus, but I've come too far. We've come too far, Jovi, and I'm finding it harder and harder to be without you. And it's scary and confusing, but nothing is more terrifying than the thought of losing you, so I'd rather feel love in your arms than not feel you at all."

Heat expanded through me, as if a star was being born in my chest. I wrapped my arms around her and brought her body closer, so I could feel her heart thundering, echoing the cataclysmic effects that her words had on me. Our mouths met, as if for the first time, soft and warm and hungry.

The emotion of rediscovering one another, openly in love and unwilling to ever let go, was exhilarating. Sure, we'd kissed before, passionately and unapologetically. But it didn't compare to how our lips felt with our souls bared. I could feel her, her every atom in friction as my arms encircled her waist.

I was overwhelmed, but I couldn't afford a single second

without feeling her, without our mouths, our bodies, and our souls connected.

Happiness coursed through me like a raging river, now knowing that she felt the same way about me. I was in love with her, and she was in love with me.

It was all I could focus on. The joy of experiencing her like that was an open blossom tickling my senses and setting fires I could no longer control.

I lost myself in her kiss, as she brought her arms up around my neck and tightened her grip on me. She didn't want to let go either.

FIELD

Aida was exhausted after the last Oracle session, so I let her sleep it off while I trained outside. I couldn't fly out anymore since the Destroyers had been instructed to capture me, but I figured I could at least increase my physical strength and burn some energy in the process to avoid going stir crazy.

I was on my third set of handstands when I saw Aida's feet in front of me in the grass.

I pushed myself off the ground and landed on my feet, to find her standing there in a pale orange linen dress, most likely something worn under 19th century outfits as an undergarment. The fabric stretched gently over her curves, and the midsummer breeze brushed against it, showing me the lines of her legs and her generous hips. She was a wonderful sight to behold, even in someone else's clothes.

My throat felt dry, and all I was able to do was nod my hello to her.

She gave me a lazy but bright smile. She'd just woken up, judging by her sleepy eyes and tousled cascade of brown and golden hair.

"Can we go up on the roof?" she asked, her cheeks blushing. "The wind's a little stronger up there. It's getting really hot here, and I'd like to cool down a little."

"Say no more." I beamed at her.

I loved holding her in my arms, and I especially enjoyed flying with her, even if it was just from the ground to the roof of an old plantation house. I whisked her off her feet, feeling her soft and warm against my chest, and spread my wings. I flapped them several times before our toes touched the roof tiles.

We sat down on the far western end, our feet dangling in the air as we watched the Destroyers move around the protective shield, patrolling quietly. Goren occasionally barked orders at them, and some rolled their yellow eyes, but they all obeyed.

"How are you feeling?" I asked her.

"I'm okay, I think." She shrugged, giving me a weak smile. "I haven't experienced any other Oracle transformation symptoms lately. I'm starting to think that these runes appearing during my visions are the worst thing that's going to happen. I'm hoping it stops there!"

"Tell me if you experience anything else," I replied. "I'm not easily scared."

"That you certainly aren't." She chuckled, then looked down

at the Destroyers again, frowning. "I wonder what they keep doing down there, wandering around the shield. They obviously can't get in."

The creatures were checking the soil where the protective shield started, using the tips of their spears to dig in. I looked around and noticed they were doing the same all around.

"Maybe they're looking for the perfect spots to plant their explosive charges," I mused.

She looked at me, her eyes wide.

"Do you think they can get through with those?"

"I doubt it," I shook my head. "As long as we have the Daughter here, her sisters would never let Azazel through."

"You heard Vita. Azazel has a Daughter in his possession as well. From what our Daughter told us, based on the conversation with her sisters, that bastard has leverage over them. What if he figures out this is their doing and demands action from them?"

I thought about it for a while, remembering the Daughter's account of her sisters' words.

"I don't know. I'm thinking maybe they wouldn't, but that's just my opinion," I said slowly.

"Why not?"

"They've already made a deal with him not to intervene in his conquest of Eritopia. Technically speaking, they actually didn't when they placed this mansion under the shield. They were only protecting their sister. At least that's how I see it."

"Let's hope your reasoning is true." She sighed, then leaned into me, resting her head on my shoulder. "I should focus my next visions on the Destroyers again. I'll bet I've yet to discover all the juicy stuff we could use against them."

I smiled, resting my head on hers in response. She never ceased to amaze me. Always so proactive, so ready to fight and try harder to get results. I breathed her scent in, and her soft hair tickled my jaw.

Once all this was over, I was determined to give her everything she wanted, everything she needed, and more. She'd wrestled with her self-esteem for so long that I'd made it my mission to get her to see herself through my eyes, because she was gorgeous and strong and a force to be reckoned with.

I felt her go limp and slide down. I caught her before she fell off the roof and held her tight. Her head fell back, and I saw her eyes roll white as runes started to flicker across her skin. She was having a vision, and I wasn't sure she'd planned it.

Her breathing was even, and her body was tender in my hands. Even in this state, I couldn't get enough of Aida. I was ready to kill anyone who tried to take her away from me.

The bond we shared ran deeper than I'd originally thought. My heart swelled at the mere thought of her. I felt acutely that all roads would lead to her in the end. We were meant to be.

I was thinking about the Destroyers one minute, and the next I was walking among them, beyond the shield. I froze at first, wondering how I'd ended up there, but when none of them saw or heard me, I realized I was having a vision.

I sighed and shook my head in disappointment. I was having a good moment with Field, and this vision had caught me unprepared.

I looked over my shoulder, where the mansion was supposed to be, but I couldn't see anything because of the protective shield. I stood on the very edge, where three Destroyers were checking the ground with their swords, stabbing it here and there.

I leaned forward to peek through the shield, and I saw myself up on the roof, limp in Field's arms. I felt a grin stretching on my face as butterflies tickled my stomach, pleased to see him looking after me.

I turned to face the Destroyers again, watching as they poked the ground, muttering and hissing among themselves. Goren barked more orders several yards behind us.

"I don't get it," one of the creatures said.

"Get what?" asked the second.

"How a weakling like Azazel managed to amass so much power. Genevieve and Almus alone could have taken him down if they put their heads together. Not to mention the other kingdoms. I still don't get how he made it this far."

"We all know he's got some dirty secrets up his sleeve," the third Destroyer chimed in. "This spell he has us under, it's not of Druid making."

"I can't even kill myself," the first one muttered.

"He won't let you. He needs us."

"For what? He's already got so much power! He's about to overtake the last planet, and his dark magic is ridiculously strong," the second one said.

"He's not as strong as you think, though."

That got my full attention.

"What do you mean, Uvar?" the second Destroyer replied.

"You've heard the rumors. You hear the others whispering in the dark. He still has a soft spot for that Lamia, and he's too proud to admit it. He was too proud to even admit there's another Druid out there standing, even when we all saw him in the castle. Under his nose! He's losing his touch. He can't focus because of Tamara," Uvar whispered, constantly looking over his shoulder to make sure Goren couldn't hear him.

"You think?"

"Yes," he nodded vehemently. "He's been pining after her since she ran away with his child. I'm not sure whether he wants her back or just wants both her and the little Lamia dead, though. His pride is of epic proportions. Makes him do the cruelest things."

A moment passed before either of them spoke again. They continued testing the ground further along the shield.

"I'm still having a hard time believing Azazel was ever a Druid," the first Destroyer said.

"That's because you were only a child when he went dark and lost his Druid form, Garnet," Uvar replied. "You didn't meet him when they assigned him the third planet. He had great plans, much ambition. He was progressive, a lover of mixing sciences with magic, but the bureaucracy drove him off the edge. He couldn't get anything done, and his pride couldn't take so many defeats. He just lost it."

"Well," the second Destroyer said, "we both know it wasn't just the bureaucracy that made him flip."

Uvar snickered, wiping beads of sweat from his forehead. Garnet looked at them both, visibly confused.

"What's Keiten talking about?" he asked.

Garnet grinned. "They didn't tell you anything, huh?"

"Azazel had the hots for Genevieve, but she kept shooting him down. Not only did she reject his advances, but she married Almus, once Azazel's closest friend. Then she sided with the other Druids and kicked him down every time he made significant changes to his kingdom's legislation. I think he truly lost it when he got word of her pregnancy. He loved and hated her at the same time, because she had enough power and influence to keep him in his little corner. But then she died in childbirth, and Azazel was suddenly on a roll."

I would've stayed for longer, but my vision had decided I'd had enough. I scoffed as I slipped into darkness, making a mental note to find a way to control timing on these sessions. It was getting frustrating.

I could feel myself moving, as another image came into focus. I realized I was walking alongside Patrik, somewhere in the dungeons of Azazel's castle. The black stone walls were narrow and glistening under the green torches.

We entered one of the prison halls, where hundreds of cages were stacked on top of each other in multiple rows. I recognized several fae, Lamias, a couple of other species I'd yet to recognize, and a plethora of incubi and succubi. They all looked miserable and wounded. Their clothes were tattered, and their shackles bit into their ankles and wrists.

Patrik was quiet as he slithered forward, walking between two rows, his yellow eyes wandering as the creatures he passed shuddered and backed into their cages in a desperate attempt to put some distance between themselves and the Destroyer.

He stopped in front of a Lamia's cage. The torn silk dress she wore had once been bright red. Now it was faded and covered in dried blood and dirt. Her snake eyes were a gold yellow, and the scales on her long arms, legs, and neck were smooth and a familiar shade of greenish yellow. Her hair was long and straight, a cold platinum shade that reminded me of someone.

"Tamara," I said to myself. "You look a lot like Tamara."

I got closer to the cage to get a better look. Patrik watched her for a while. She glared at him, her lips twisted with disgust.

"You can keep coming here until the world ends," she muttered. "I will never tell you where she is."

"Kyana, I'm not asking for Azazel. I've told you before. Unfortunately, I can't convince you otherwise, given my condition, but I still have to know. Where is your sister?" Patrik's voice was calm and low.

"I don't know."

"You must know something. You must know where she's hiding. Azazel is intensifying his search for her, and she must be warned. Where is Tamara?" he insisted.

She scoffed and rolled her eyes. I liked her spunk.

"I have no idea. And I would never tell you. You said yes to him. You said yes!" She was seething, and I started to get a feeling that there had been some history between them. The pained look on his face and her blistering anger pointed to it.

"You know I had no choice, Kyana," he replied, his voice

trembling. "Please, just tell me where Tamara is. I need to reach out to her before he finds her. I don't want him to win, but there isn't much I can do to fight him. He's still in control of my will, but I've been able to shut down his hold on me for brief moments. I can help her. I can help you both see each other again."

Kyana's glare did not subside.

"What happened between the two of you?" I asked out loud, although I knew I wouldn't get an answer.

"What happened to you, Patrik?" she muttered, her gaze softening slightly. "You had everything. You had me. And then you said yes to Azazel. Why did you do that?"

"You know exactly why I did it," he shot back, grunting. He was struggling with self-control again.

"What? He threatened to kill me? Well, he put me in a cage, instead. Well done, Patrik. I would've been better off dead, and you would've fought against him a little while longer. Maybe you would've even made a difference!"

Patrik grasped the cage bars, drops of sweat sliding down his temples. There was a mixture of pain and longing in his yellow eyes, as they flickered back to his natural color for a moment—enough for Kyana to notice and get closer.

"I'm not letting you die, Kyana," he replied. "I'm meaningless without you."

He reached into the cage, slowly, and his knuckles brushed her cheek gently. She smiled. Then she hissed and bit into his hand, her fangs piercing the skin, drawing blood.

He cursed and withdrew his hand, taking a step back.

She chuckled and spat the blood to her side, licking her lips with a sadistic grin. "You're already meaningless, you mindless beast. You're Azazel's puppet," Kyana said.

Patrik's eyes changed back to yellow, as he gripped his wound with two fingers and slithered out of the dungeon. There was more than physical pain carved into his features. He was suffering tremendously because of his situation and because of the rift that Azazel had put between him and Kyana.

Clearly Druids and Lamias didn't get along very well, despite the Lamias' procreation needs, but Patrik and Kyana seemed to have been in a relationship before Azazel came along. It made sense to me, in a way. They descended from the Druid species, and they had more in common with them than with any other creature. And the Lamias were beautiful. There was plenty to fall for.

Kyana watched as he disappeared into the corridor, left in utter silence with just the sound of water dripping somewhere nearby. She wiped the blood from her lips with the back of her hand before she caved in and shuddered. Sobbing tears streamed down her cheeks. I felt sorry for her, trapped in there, forced to watch her lover turn into a beast.

I stood on a massive platform made of black marble with archways stretching across it. Glass bubbles hung from them, most of them empty. I was at the top level of Azazel's castle, where he kept his collection of Oracles. He was on the edge, looking up at Destroyers atop their winged horses as they circled above. My blood ran cold.

I gasped as I recognized the Nevertide Oracle floating in one of them. Two more were prisoners there, both females who were blind and covered in runes. I walked toward them, and, as I stopped in front of the Nevertide Oracle, she opened her white eyes.

My breath hitched.

"Aida," I heard her whispering inside my head.

I froze, realizing that she could see me.

"Aida, there isn't much time," she said, her lips still. "There's a traitor among you."

"Wait, what? How? No, that's not possible," I said.

My mind instantly started going over all possible scenarios, looking at every single person in our group, every ally and new friend made, including the succubi, the Dearghs, and the Lamias. I shook my head.

"Azazel is cunning, Aida," the Nevertide Oracle insisted. "His spells will slither into one's soul, and you won't even know he's looking or listening. You must be careful. I see betrayal hanging over your heads."

"You don't know what you're saying!" I shot back. "Besides, why should I believe you? You're stuck here with him! I know he can control the visions. What if what you're telling me now is actually coming from Azazel, just trying to cause a divide between us?"

"Aida, please believe me! I didn't give you my gift to see you end up here in a glass bubble. I'm trying to help you," she pleaded, placing her palm on the glass, as if reaching out to me.

I didn't believe her in the slightest, but before I could say anything else, the image warped before my eyes, and Azazel burst out of nowhere, his face inches from mine with big eyes blazing green and a chilling grin stretching from ear to ear.

"Gotcha!" he hissed, and I screamed.

I screamed as hard as my lungs could handle.

I woke up, still screaming with my arms flailing. Field's arms held me tight to keep me from falling.

I gasped and cried as I looked around, realizing I was back on the roof.

"Aida, I'm here. It's okay!" Field said, his hands gripping my shoulders.

Horror filled my veins with ice, and my stomach reduced itself to the size of a pea.

"Aida, it's okay."

It took me a minute or two before I was able to speak again, my eyes darting around as if expecting to see Azazel pop out again somehow.

"He saw me," I managed to croak. "Field, he saw me! Azazel saw me!"

He stilled, his turquoise eyes nearly popping out of their orbits.

"How? How? How did he see you? What happened?"

I burst into tears, shuddering as he pulled me into a comforting embrace.

"I was on top of his castle. The Nevertide Oracle was there. She could see me, but this wasn't the first time. She's done it with Vita, too, so I was surprised, but not shocked. And...and..."

I cried and hiccupped and tried to pull myself together.

"She was trying to plant doubt in my mind, trying to convince me that there's a traitor among us, and then...and then he showed up, out of nowhere! He said 'Gotcha!' and I screamed and woke up."

Field kept quiet, listening as I wept and recounted my vision. I found warmth and comfort in his arms, enough to help me regain my composure as I wiped the tears from my eyes and looked up at him. My spine was stiff, riddled with chills.

"He saw me... I don't know how he did it, but he saw me. He knows I'm here now. He knows there's an Oracle here."

It wouldn't have taken a lot for Azazel to suspect there was an Oracle hiding beneath the protective shield, given that he'd already sensed us when we were first transported to Eritopia. But having absolute certainty brought on a whole new level of trouble, giving him the extra motivation to get past the spell.

I couldn't fathom the lengths he would be willing to go to in order to capture me now that he'd seen me. The stakes were immeasurably higher when an Oracle was the grand prize. I wondered whether Azazel would be able to breach the shield by using the young Daughter he had in his possession. He hadn't done it up to that point, so perhaps it didn't work that way.

29

SERENA

The incubi had already gathered around us too quickly for any of us to draw our weapons in time. Sverik's words regarding their scouting and assault prowess rang loud in my head. Jax was faster, though, his eyes glowing yellow as he subdued our attackers. They fell to their knees, whimpering and crying, stricken with inexplicable grief.

"No, please stop! Don't do this! No!" one of them sobbed, clutching his head as he collapsed on his side.

"What did you do to them?" I asked, goosebumps tickling my skin. I still gripped my sword in its sheath.

"I made them see something they did not wish to see," Jax replied. "Destroyers torturing them."

I looked at them, lying in the sand in a fetal position, moaning and weeping. It gave us the window we needed to spur our horses onward and reach the settlement, where hundreds of incubi were waiting with their weapons drawn.

Sverik raised his arms in the air, in a defensive gesture.

The rogues pointed their swords and arrows at us. Campfires blazed behind them.

"We come in peace!" Sverik said.

"What do you want?" One of them stepped forward, his knuckles white as he held a long spear in his hands. The metal tip glistened purple, reminding me of the poisons the succubi laced their arrows with.

I heard them all grumbling as their feet shuffled through the sand. There was fear in their eyes but also determination. They were on the defensive, and they would not go down easy if we were to attack. Our mission was to establish an alliance. We just had to get past the poisoned spears and swords.

"It's me, Sverik! Kristos's brother!"

A moment of tense silence flickered by, before another incubus spoke from the crowd.

"And?"

"What do you mean 'And'?" Sverik was irritated, hands still up. "Come on, Grezzi! I'm here to help! We're here to help!"

"Why should I trust the son of Arid after he sided with Azazel?" The incubus identified as Grezzi stepped in front of the group, two large swords poised to strike us down in a heartbeat.

"Because I'm not involved with Azazel anymore. I had no

choice but to follow my father after Kristos died," Sverik shot back. "Then I was thrown in a cage. These people saved me!"

Grezzi's crystal blue eyes darted from Sverik to Draven and me, then to Jax and Hansa. He processed the information for a minute or so, with a permanent frown on his face. He measured us carefully.

"Who are these people?" he eventually asked.

"I'm Draven, a Dru—"

"A Druid. Yeah, I can tell. I'm not blind. Just like I can tell he's a Mara and she's a succubus. How are you not slithering around yet? You've not met Azazel?" Grezzi didn't seem patient by nature.

"I have. Just once," Draven replied. "I'm the son of Almus and Genevieve. And these are my allies."

Grezzi put his swords down, his shoulders dropping with relief. The weapons seemed heavy, judging by the expression on his face. "Allies for what?"

"We're going to war. We're taking Azazel down," I said, capturing his attention, and, based on the grin slitting his face, his interest.

Grezzi ordered his incubi to put their weapons away. He learned our names and where we came from. He tried using his natural abilities on me—my head felt light and my skin rippled—but Draven was quick to cut him off.

"I'd like to kindly ask you to stop what you're doing to her," he said, his voice cold and sharp as a blade. "And don't think of trying it again."

"Or else what?" Grezzi shot back with a smirk.

"Or else she'll take over your mind and tear you apart from the inside," was Draven's blunt reply, making me grin.

They took us inside the camp, where a large bonfire burned bright and orange. Their tents were small and rectangular with furs and spotted skins hung on the sides. A few animals were being roasted, reminding me that I hadn't eaten much during the day.

We followed Grezzi into his tent, while the other incubi returned to their posts. His temporary home was larger than the others, complete with a makeshift bed and a table, where old maps were spread out. Small wooden figurines rested on top in strategic places. Based on how the pieces were arranged across the map, he'd been following Azazel's expansion from afar.

"And Bijarki is with you, you say?" Grezzi asked as we gathered around the table.

Draven nodded. "I've been working with him for quite some time now. He brought Kristos into the fold."

"You know, I don't get it. Where have you been all this time? Why hasn't Azazel killed you?"

"He didn't know I existed until a couple of days ago. My father kept me hidden and safe. My home is under the Daughters' protection."

"And your father?"

A shadow passed over Draven's face. "Dead," he replied. "We'd been rescuing Oracles, keeping them out of Azazel's reach. He died trying to save one."

Grezzi nodded, his gaze moving around, measuring each of us from head to toe before settling on the map. "So, tell me, Druid. Why should we side with you, then? We've been surviving here quite well on our own." He poured water into a silver goblet, which he gulped down.

"Do you want to keep surviving, or do you want to live?"

Draven's answer made the incubus smile.

"Fair enough. What are you bringing into this fight? I'm not getting my incubi killed for a young and inexperienced Druid without a plan and some serious war power."

"I have three Oracles and the support of the Daughters."

"The Daughters," Grezzi scoffed. "Like they even care anymore."

"It turns out they do, just a little. Otherwise I wouldn't have survived until now. It's better than nothing," Draven replied. "The Dearghs, the Lamias, the Maras, and the Tritones have joined as well, along with the Red Tribe and a few other essential players."

He gave me a sideways glance as he said that, and I tried hard not to smile. My heart filled with pride. It felt good to be acknowledged in front of such war-seasoned creatures as an important element in this fight against Azazel. It was one thing to hear Draven tell me such things in the privacy of our conversations, but it was something else entirely when I was described as essential to what seemed like an efficient army of incubi.

"Do you have a plan?" Grezzi asked.

"We need more bodies first. I need to make sure we can count on you. I've arranged for us to meet in seven moons at the northern waterfall of Mount Agrith. If you agree, I can let the others know, and we can form an alliance against Azazel. The Tritones and the Dearghs are already out rallying more creatures. We have enough power and strength between us to leave Azazel without his armies. And, with the Oracles' help, we can bring him to his knees, once and for all."

"He has Oracles too, doesn't he?"

"He does. But they never told him about me. I don't think they're quite as helpful to him as he thinks. There's a window of opportunity there, and we want to use it, before he catches on."

Grezzi nodded slowly, his finger moving along the map. I glanced at it and noticed he was following a trail from his camp to Mount Agrith. Judging by the distance between the two points and the memory I had of the map in Draven's study, I realized that we'd made it very far northeast of the mansion. This planet was huge, and I'd barely seen a fraction of it. There must be plenty of rogues out there hiding in the thousands of square miles of thick jungles.

"Azazel has tens of thousands of incubi in his army, and at least five hundred Destroyers at the last count," Grezzi said, his eyes on the obsidian figurine of Azazel on the map, resting on the location of his castle. Someone had made the effort to carve a realistic figure of him, with a swirling snake lower body and an insidious grin. "How many do you think you have in your alliance so far?"

"Numbers are not what will help us win this war," Draven replied. "We have massive tactical advantages and the swamp witches' books. There's a great amount of magic in them that Azazel has yet to discover. Our Oracles have been uncovering secrets from Azazel's past, weaknesses among his Destroyers, and, most importantly, we know what the future holds and have been able to change it with our actions. Granted, the changes haven't been very encouraging, but an alliance with the rogue nations will get us the scale-tipping result we need. We can corner this bastard if we play our cards right."

"Then why do you need us if you don't need numbers?" the incubus asked.

"Are you fine with just sitting here until it's all over, or would you like to pitch in?" Sverik interjected. "Your scouts are known for their ability to cover large territories in short periods of time. We need them to spread the word, find more rogues, and bring them into the alliance. Then you can join the fight as well. Your troops are impressive."

Grezzi straightened his back, overflowing with pride. Sverik had managed to hit a soft spot.

"I must say, I agree," Jax noticed his play and went along. "Neither of us saw your scouts coming earlier. They are exceptionally well-trained. I must apologize for their agony, though. They should recover soon. Just give them a lot of water."

The incubus sucked his teeth, then slapped both hands on the table.

"They'll be fine," he replied. "They should've spotted the Mara in the group, anyway. Whatever happened, it's on them."

He then looked at us once more, squinting his eyes when his gaze reached me.

"I'll send my boys out to get you more soldiers," he said. "And I will meet you in seven moons at Mount Agrith, as per your request."

A wave of relief washed over me.

Draven nodded respectfully. "Thank you, Grezzi. We need as many of them as you can rally by the seventh moon. And bring their leaders to the northern waterfall. We'll sign a pact there," he replied.

"Make it a blood pact," the incubus shot back. "And if I get the faintest whiff of foul play, I will make sure nobody gets on your boat. I may be reduced to a small garrison here in the middle of nowhere, but I still have a reputation to uphold."

"That's perfectly understandable," Sverik replied. "Thank you nonetheless. Your support is essential."

Grezzi nodded, then let out a sharp whistle. A couple of seconds later, ten young incubi came into the tent wearing dark green military uniforms. They stood straight, waiting for his order.

"Get ready, boys. We're going to war. Rally the rogues all over the continent, spread out far and wide, and leave no stone unturned. There are plenty of tribes and deserter camps out there. Send them a message from me, and, if they agree, bring their leaders to me by the sixth moon," he said.

The incubi nodded firmly.

Grezzi pulled a piece of parchment, a small ink bottle, and a quill from a side table behind him. He wrote something down and handed the parchment to one of the scouts.

"Have copies of this ready. At least twenty. I want you to come back with none," he added.

The young scout nodded again, then swiftly left the tent, followed by the other nine.

I was impressed by how responsive and disciplined his soldiers were. We could certainly use them in an assault if we gave them the right weapons and spells against Destroyers. They were well-organized and swift on their feet, both key qualities in a war with Azazel's monsters.

Grezzi raised his hands and smiled.

"We're just about to sit down and eat. Would you like to join us?" he asked. "I can have a couple of tents ready for you by the time dinner is done. It's best for you to travel back in the morning. Plenty of evil things in the woods at night."

My stomach's muffled growls caught his attention, as well as Draven's.

"That sounds good, thank you," the Druid replied for me.

After we ate, we were escorted to two tents. Draven stepped forward, taking my hand as he went inside one of them.

"Hansa, you can share the other with Jax and Sverik, can't you?" he asked over his shoulder, without waiting for a reply.

I heard her mutter something unsavory, but we were already inside, where a thick layer of furs and blankets awaited and a small oil lamp burned in a corner.

"Are you sure she'll be okay there?" I asked.

Draven looked at me, his expression firm and difficult to read, and started taking off his boots. "She'll be fine. I'd be more worried about Jax and Sverik. They're the ones stuck in there with her," he quipped, giving me his nonchalant smirk.

I laughed lightly and slipped out of my boots, suddenly aware that I was in there alone with Draven. My self-consciousness crashed into me. My nerves began to tingle at the thought of being so close to him in a tent that we had all to ourselves.

A dozen thoughts started buzzing through my head, raising my temperature as I set the boots aside and stood in front of him not sure of what to do next. He looked up at me, a familiar warmth in his gray eyes. His fingers grasped the belt I'd used to fasten my borrowed trousers and pulled me closer.

He sat in front of me on a mound of soft furs, his head at the same level as my abdomen and his gaze fixed on mine.

My breath hitched as he put on a mischievous smile, gripped my hips, and jerked me toward him. I squealed as I fell on top of him on the makeshift bed and giggled as his arms circled my waist and kept me tight against his hard body.

His scent invaded my nostrils, the same whiff of musk and sunshine I'd grown happily accustomed to. We looked at each other for a minute, as our emotions flared. I felt his intense heat and golden energy pouring through me, and I opened my soul for him in return.

I kissed him, softly at first, enough to get a taste of him.

"I wasn't kidding earlier," he whispered. "You were unbelievable today. You're unbelievable every day, and yet you still manage to surprise me."

I gave him another kiss, as sweet and delicate as the first one. Heat coursed through my veins. His mouth opened, demanding every ounce of passion that flooded my mind and soul.

I abandoned my senses and deepened the kiss, giving him more. His hands moved up my back, fingers pressing against my muscles. A sigh ripped from my chest. He groaned and paused for a second, his eyes hooded and breath ragged.

"I'm still trying to figure out how you snuck into my soul the way you did, Serena," he said. "At first I tried to think of ways to get you out."

"And now?" I asked, cupping his face with my hands.

"And now all I think of are ways of spending a moment alone with you. It becomes challenging at times."

I giggled. "Well then, consider this a raging success," I replied, kissing the tip of his nose.

He put on his most seductive smile, rolled us over, and brought his weight down on me. His leg made its way between my thighs, and his hands took mine. Our fingers intertwined. He raised our hands above my head. He kissed me, deeply and emotionally as ribbons of gold seeped into me from his very soul.

My heart thudded as he held me on the very edge of rapture. My chest was soft against his toned torso, a perfect fit. My curves matched his sharp edges with wonderful precision. He left my hands above my head and used his palms and fingers to draw delicate lines down my arms and sides, until he reached my hips and pulled them up, pressing his forward at the same time.

I exhaled hard as Draven's touch brought me closer to something I wasn't sure how to handle. Tension gathered in my lower body, and something intense fluttered in my chest, as I once more confirmed the only fact I knew for sure in this entire Eritopian affair—there was no place I'd rather be than here, with him.

Hansa's irritated voice shattered our moment from beyond the tent.

"No, no, you two can sleep there together. I can't put up with your childish bickering anymore!" she snapped.

Draven cursed under his breath and pushed himself off, rolling to the side with an irritated sigh.

"We have company," he muttered before Hansa walked in.

I was lying on my back, looking at Draven, my breath still shaky and my muscles liquid. Disappointment crushed me as I realized Draven and I were not going to spend the night alone in that tent.

"I am sorry, but Jax and Sverik are like two little children who don't like each other for no particular reason. I can't. I just can't. I have no patience for male egos," Hansa grumbled and threw herself on the bed next to me.

Draven smiled at me gently, making me feel warm and fuzzy on the inside. Nothing mattered in that moment, not even Hansa claiming one third of the only bed in that tent. My attention belonged to the Druid, who channeled a great deal of affection toward me. I felt the arousal, the sheer desire, and the frustration, but, at the same time, I felt something I'd only vaguely sensed before—something far more intense and colorful, akin to a four-letter word I was still wary of saying out loud.

"That's okay," I mumbled and turned to one side so I could face Draven better.

A few minutes later, Hansa blew out the amber flame in the oil lamp, and darkness covered us. Outside, wood still crackled in the campfire, and incubi still whispered and shuffled between tents.

Inside, I was inches away from Draven. We weren't touching, just gazing at each other with smiling eyes and tender lips. We fell asleep like that, as I wondered what the next day would bring for our alliance and for this incredible bond forming between us.

30

SERENA

W hen morning came, we packed our satchels and said goodbye to Grezzi and his incubi with a promise to see them again in six moons. The soldiers saluted us respect-fully as our horses galloped back down the white sand beach. The sun rose brightly to our left.

We'd made substantial progress, and it felt like we could actually score a win with these creatures. Grezzi, despite his general distrust of people, seemed happy to join our alliance. I had a feeling they'd been waiting there for a long time for someone to come along and offer them a better option than living in isolation on the northeastern shore while Azazel destroyed the world.

When we reached White City, the Maras watched us from inside the buildings, where darkness kept them safe. The city looked even more beautiful in the sunlight, glistening white as the salty breeze rustled the dark green leaves of the surrounding forest. The mountain it had been carved into was tall and sharp, keeping it well protected from mainland visitors.

Jax had covered himself completely. His head was protected by the black hood, and his hands were hidden in gloves. He was the first to get off his horse and go inside, motioning for us to follow him. We left our horses at the bottom of the stairs and went in after him.

He took us to the hall, where he'd hosted us the night before. Several young Maras waited there, one offering him a golden chalice filled with blood. He removed his gloves and hood and drank it hastily, licking his lips as he looked at us.

"Few creatures know how we feed," he said. "We don't socialize much with others."

"I'm not surprised," I replied. "You're quite secluded here."

"Which is why us joining your alliance is such a rare and special occurrence. I hope you can appreciate that," he said.

"We certainly do," Draven said. "I must thank you for your involvement and for coming with us last night. The conversation might have had a different outcome had it not been for your quick reaction to Grezzi's scouts."

"There's one condition to our collaboration going forward," Jax said. "And I will not take no for an answer."

I noticed a frown pulling Draven's eyebrows closer, as he waited for the Mara to state his terms.

"I need to come with you to your mansion. I need to meet your Oracles. I need to make sure everything you say is true.

Otherwise, I'm not putting my people at further risk. It's all nice and good that Grezzi agreed to help, but I cannot bring myself to get involved without palpable evidence."

Draven and I looked at each other for a long moment. Even though he'd helped us so far, it was still hard for us to fully trust someone to the point of bringing them into the shield. We'd already made a massive concession with the Lamias, and, given the current circumstances, we were stuck with them.

I then looked at Hansa, whose emerald-gold eyes were fixed on Jax. Her expression was firm and difficult to read, but the way her eyes sparked told me there was a level of interest there. Sverik rolled his eyes and exhaled loudly, prompting the Mara to shift his gaze to him and raise an eyebrow.

"If that's what it takes to earn your trust, then so be it. But I must advise that if you come with us, you cannot withdraw from this agreement. If you do, it will cost you your life," Draven replied, his voice cold and unyielding.

Jax cocked his head, visibly intrigued.

"Once we let you in, you'll be privy to extremely sensitive information," Draven added. "We cannot afford you walking out knowing all of that and not being on our side. Our lives would be at risk. Our entire mission would be in jeopardy."

Jax thought this over for a while, then nodded at the young Maras waiting quietly by the wall. They gave him a curt nod and shuffled out of the hall. He half-smiled at us.

"Fair enough. Something tells me there's more in that mansion of yours than just Oracles and swamp witch spells that you're so protective of, which is fine. Now I'm even more curious. You have a deal, Druid."

Draven's main concern was the Daughter, and we both knew it, as did Hansa and Sverik, given the looks they gave us. We couldn't bring her up while still in White City, but once we brought him to the mansion, Jax would see for himself why we hadn't been fully forthcoming about our tactical advantages.

Jax was still quite the mystery to me, and since Draven had mentioned killing him if he betrayed us, I wondered how that could be done. Vampires were immortal and could only be killed by the sun, UV-ray guns, or a stake through the heart. Jax had mentioned being around for millennia, but did that mean the Maras were immortal as well? I knew the sun could kill them and that silver was highly toxic to them, but were there any other means by which a Mara could be permanently executed?

He'd been helpful so far, and we did have a lot of things in common—not just because of Azazel but also due to the fact that his species was similar to our vampires back home. But at the same time, I felt like I hadn't come close enough to trusting him yet. I made a mental note to ask Draven how a Mara could be killed, just in case.

Jax put on his fighting gear to come with us back to the

mansion. When he rejoined us in the hall, I found myself staring.

He was already tall and well-built, but the equipment made him seem even taller. Black leather covered him from head to toe with thin laces on the sides to tighten the fabric around his broad chest and narrow hips. Metallic plates dyed black and lacquered to a smooth finish were mounted on his shins, calves, arms, and torso, interconnected through a fine mesh for mobility. The suit came with a pair of simple black boots, black gloves with metallic knuckles, a mask that completely covered his head, and a pair of smoky goggles.

Hansa couldn't take her eyes off him. She stood in awe of his weaponry and equipment as he stepped forward and mounted a pair of long swords on his back. I noticed mesh beneath the plates used over his mouth and nose to make it easier for him to breathe and a black metal plate hanging around his neck, molded to fit his mandible in case he needed to protect it.

"That is so cool," I gasped as he stopped in front of me and Hansa.

Hansa nodded her approval.

"Like it?" he quipped. "Made it myself. We've been using these in combat for centuries. It's one of the reasons the others stay away from us. We used to be confined to the dark hours of the day, but ever since we started using these, we've been able to fight in broad daylight. It's turned the tables in our favor."

"It looks like it can take a few hits as well," Hansa said, gaze fixed on his chest.

The black metal plates had an intricate design engraved onto their surface, forming a sort of emblem on his torso with fine curves and leafy patterns on the edges.

"More than a few," he replied. "This is dragon bone."

Hansa's eyes grew wide with admiration, as she ran her fingers down the chest plate.

"What's dragon bone?" I asked. *Is there a species of dragon in Eritopia?*

"It's an extremely rare metal," she explained absently. "Only found in mines beneath the volcanoes these days. Very difficult to forge and work into something so fine and light."

Jax nodded then broke contact. One of his young servants handed him his weapons, and he mounted them on his suit one by one. There were several knives, and two pouches with small triangular blades, perfect for throwing.

He then turned to face us once more, arms extended to his sides.

"Well, what are we waiting for? Let's go," he said.

He bid his farewells to his fellow Maras, then went outside. We followed.

There were two canoes waiting in the water: our special ride from Zeriel and a long black one for Jax. We got in and paddled our way back to the lagoon.

I sat at the front with Draven behind me, followed by Hansa and Sverik, who were doing the paddling. The ocean was a deep dark blue under a clear sky. The rocky coast glided by as we returned to the lagoon.

The Tritones' home opened up to us in a beautiful shade of turquoise. The water was as superb and clear as ever. Some of them were swimming or basking in the sunlight, while others were foraging through the surrounding rainforest for fruit and nuts. The foragers returned with full wicker baskets and placed them under the shade of a massive palm tree.

As soon as our canoe reached the shore, I heard splashing behind us. I got out and reached for my waterproof satchel, but I was suddenly grabbed and pulled into the water. With my head under, my first instinct was to push out a barrier in self-defense. A split second before I did so, I saw Zeriel swimming around me, grinning like a mischievous child.

I instantly regretted not being able to affect his mind, as I was awfully tempted to make him do ridiculous things and embarrass him in front of his Tritones. Instead, I swam back to the shore and walked out, cursing under my breath.

Draven came next to me with a baffled expression on his face.

"Are you okay? You were in front of me and then you vanished in the water. I didn't have time to react before you popped out again," he said.

I felt his concern and fear dripping through me and instantly calmed down, eager to soothe his emotions. I placed my hand on his chest and gave him a warm smile, then pointed at the water.

"Zeriel's a big kid with a crown. That's all I'm going to say," I muttered and put a few more yards between myself and the water.

Zeriel came out, laughing lightly as his tail morphed into legs. An innocent look graced his face.

"Oh, come on! I was just playing, Serena!"

Draven glared at him, his eyes flickering black. I knew the Tritone was just being playful, but he'd already gotten on the Druid's nerves with his flirtatious demeanor several times. As soon as the irritation subsided, I was tempted to laugh, but I decided to defuse the potential conflict, as I felt Draven's anger pouring out of him.

"Careful not to lose an eye in the process," I replied, then looked around at the other Tritones, all stilled and watching with concern etched into their beautiful features. "Don't think I'm in any way intimidated by your royal status. If you want to play rough, I will play rough, and you'll be the only one bruised."

Zeriel stifled a laugh and bowed in apology, his gaze shifting from me to Draven. He offered the Druid his hand as a gesture of peace, still biting into his lower lip to prevent a grin from stretching all over his face.

"I apologize to you both," he said.

Draven sighed and shook his hand, and Zeriel finally laughed and slapped him on the shoulder.

"That's the spirit!" he exclaimed, then looked up at the passage stone. "So! What's the plan? My Tritones are out in the water world gathering the other tribes of our nation. Did you reach out to the incubi?"

Sverik nodded, beaming with satisfaction.

"We most certainly did. We'll meet on the sixth moon at Mount Agrith, like we agreed," the incubus replied.

"His scouts are now reaching out to other rogues on the mainland," Draven added. "We'll now be going back to the mansion. We're surrounded by Destroyers and need to make sure we hold out until the meeting."

Zeriel nodded firmly, putting on his serious face.

"Good. Well done, then. We'll prepare for Mount Agrith in the meantime."

"Just watch out for Sluaghs and green fireflies," I warned him. "The Sluaghs are working with Azazel, and the fireflies are a spy spell. They see and hear everything."

Zeriel gave me his nonchalant smirk, hands on his hips. "Worry not. We'll be careful. Thank you, Serena."

He then guided us up a narrow path that led us to the passage stone. Zeriel gave us each a farewell hug. He spent an extra minute holding me, much to Draven's discontent.

"This Druid is simply mad about you," the Tritone whispered in my ear. "He is ridiculously lucky to have your affection. I hope you know that."

I smiled at him. "I think it goes both ways."

He grinned, then looked at Draven.

"Worry not, Druid. I have no intention of taking this gorgeous creature from you. I can tell when a heart belongs to someone else, but I must say, it is so much fun messing with you!" Zeriel chuckled, then moved on to give Jax a hug.

The Mara smacked him over the head, keeping the Tritone at a safe distance. I worked hard to keep myself from laughing out loud, as Zeriel looked at him, befuddlement written all over his face.

"Just make sure you don't get killed," Jax said. "I've grown accustomed to our Pyrope, and I'm in no mood to find another sucker to take your place."

Zeriel threw his head back, laughing. "I shall miss you too, Jaxxon," he replied, then looked at Draven and me. "See you at Mount Agrith."

Draven nodded and used a small knife to draw blood from his finger. He placed his hand on the stone's smooth surface, which began to ripple. He took my hand, I took Hansa's, and she completed the connection with Sverik and Jax.

We walked through the stone.

I welcomed the cool darkness for a moment as we left the northwestern coast and instantly traveled back to the mansion. On one hand, I was excited at the thought of reuniting with my brother and friends and imagined the looks on their faces when they saw us coming back in one piece. On the other, I was worried about what we would find there, given Vita's ominous vision. I just prayed that the mansion would be there for us to come back to.

It was already afternoon when I went outside again. A reddish sky loomed over the mansion. The vision session had taken its toll on me, and I'd needed a few hours to rest and clear my head.

I walked along the shield for a while, keeping a safe distance of several feet, watching as Goren continued trying to breach it with his sword. He should've known by then that his weapons were useless against it, and yet he didn't seem to know when to stop. Judging by the angry look on his face, he was focused on letting some steam out as he grunted with each hit, squinting when golden sparks jumped from the sudden contact between his steel and the Daughters' spell.

I wondered whether they would be able to do anything with the explosive charges once they arrived. But that wasn't the worst thing on my radar. I'd just heard from Aida that Azazel had seen her through one of her visions and that the Nevertide Oracle had warned her about a traitor among us.

How was that possible? Exactly what power did Azazel hold over the Nevertide Oracle, and how many of her attempts to reach out to us had been genuine and not controlled by the King of Destroyers? Most importantly, what was the true extent of his power, given the leverage he had over the Daughters?

The fact that he had one of their sisters made the Destroyer invasion seem more likely to happen, but, at the same time, they'd put the shield in place to protect the last Daughter. I was inclined to believe that they were more likely to protect us in return for keeping her safe than to help Azazel breach the shield and capture her as well.

The notion of a traitor among us also rattled me. Who could it be? Who could Azazel control, with or without their knowledge? I had a hard time thinking it was one of mine—Aida, Jovi, Serena, Field, and Phoenix couldn't possibly be involved...even unknowingly.

My mind wandered to Draven, then Bijarki, and my heart tightened in my chest. I thought of the other succubi and the Lamias, or the incubi, even the Daughter. None seemed like a potential traitor. They'd all suffered tremendously because of Azazel. None had reasons to do such a horrible thing. And yet, maybe one of us was under his spell. Maybe one of us didn't even know we were helping him. The thought spooked me.

I took a deep breath, ran my fingers through my hair, and groaned with frustration. This wasn't getting any easier! If anything, it was spiraling further out of control, and I was struggling to stay afloat and ahead of the tide so I wouldn't be dragged under.

I stilled a couple hundred yards away from Goren. My muscles tightened as wisps of gray smoke appeared out of thin air and formed a disturbing image right in front of me, just beyond the shield.

I held my breath as I recognized the Nevertide Oracle. It was just a projection of her. She seemed submerged in water, her eyes white and runes rushing across her skin, floating above the ground.

"Vita," she spoke, deep in my head. "Vita, you have to listen to me! You're in danger!"

Ice trickled through my veins as I stood there and listened to her, a mixture of fear and anger rumbling inside my ribcage. I closed my fists at my sides, glaring at her as she continued to speak to me from beyond the shield.

"Vita, please! There isn't much time! Azazel knows there's an Oracle in there, and there was nothing I could do about it! I didn't know he was listening when I reached out to Aida. You have to believe me!"

"Why should I? If Azazel is infiltrating your visions, your abilities, why should I trust you now? How do I know it's not him talking through you as we speak?"

"He doesn't know I'm doing this, he doesn't know many things as I've kept you all from him! He suspects you might be hiding beneath the shield, but he doesn't know how to get in! Please, Vita, believe me when I tell you! You're in danger!"

I didn't move, watching her float and analyzing her words carefully.

"Who's the traitor, then?" I asked.

"I don't know yet." She shook her head slowly, her lips pursed. "I had a vision of the future, of Azazel having captured you, laughing in your face, and telling you that you were betrayed from the inside, and I've tried looking into it in past, present, and future, but my powers haven't been very helpful due to my imprisonment. I gave most of everything I had to your mother, and I'm barely left with any Oracle essence in me. It's taking its toll on me. I'm also trying to listen in on Azazel when he thinks I'm asleep, but I can't get a name out."

A few moments passed before she reached her hand out, piercing the shield and further stunning me. I didn't know how much of this was real.

"Touch my hand," she said. "Look inside me if you wish. As an Oracle, you have complete access to my being. There's a connection between Oracles—we can communicate with and see through each other freely if we learn how to reach out. It's how I'm here now, I'm projecting myself to you directly, away from visions and unbeknownst to anyone. Not even Azazel knows that, we've all kept it from him at the cost of much physical pain... Please, Vita..."

An Oracle can communicate with another Oracle outside visions?

An Oracle can touch another Oracle and see right through them? See the truth? How does that work?

I slowly raised my hand to touch hers.

I didn't even realize I was moving until our fingers touched, and I felt the cold rush through me and trickle down my spine. The view before me turned white. It was a strange vision I was having, as if I were in the Nevertide Oracle's body but with my own consciousness.

I was floating in the water bubble, feeling cold and weightless, hearing Azazel's muffled voice as he paced around my glass sphere, talking to a Destroyer.

"I don't care what you do. Find a way to get in!" he barked at the creature. "I want the Oracle, and if you come back without her, I will have your head."

My strange vision was short-lived. I felt myself fall, and everything turned white again. I hit the ground hard. Sharp pain seared my left arm and hip caused by several loose rocks. I shook my head to realize that I was lying in the dry dirt with stones digging into me.

Horror took over as I then understood that I had fallen outside the shield. I gasped as I looked back and saw my legs half-visible, the rest hidden by the Daughters' magic. I looked up and to my right, and my gaze met Goren's.

He seemed baffled for a second, before a sadistic grin slit his face. He slithered toward me, gripping his sword.

Oh, no.

I was petrified, unable to move for a split second before

adrenaline kicked in. I needed to disappear behind the shield again, where no one could see or feel me.

Feel me. Azazel can feel me outside the shield.

I pushed myself back inside the shield as the Destroyer charged toward me, hissing.

I vanished completely, and he hit the clear wall.

I breathed frantically. My eyes felt bleary as I watched Goren take his rage out on the invisible dome again, bringing his sword down and shouting all sorts of curse words.

"Come back here! Come back here, you little worm!" he barked, unable to see or hear me anymore.

My body shook, and I couldn't stop myself from crying and gasping for air. I managed to stand up and run back inside the mansion, bumping into Bijarki as I reached the foyer. He noticed my distress and instantly took me in his arms.

"Vita? What's wrong?" he asked, his brow creasing with worry.

"He saw me! The Nevertide Oracle! She appeared in front of me, and something happened, and…I fell. And he saw me!" I tried to make sense, but my words felt jumbled and difficult to extract from the back of my head.

"It's okay," he replied. "You're okay now. You're protected."

I slowly managed to get my breathing back under control, but a sense of urgency made me restless. As good as I felt in his arms, this incident added a new layer of danger to our mission and our personal safety.

I tried pushing him away, but Bijarki stood still, holding me firmly and frowning at me.

"You don't understand, Bijarki," I said, my voice trembling. "The Nevertide Oracle tried to warn me, like she tried with Aida! She touched me, somehow, and I had a vision. I was seeing what she was seeing. Azazel ordered his Destroyers to do everything possible to get us out of here. Aida was right. He knows there's an Oracle here. Except now he knows there are two of us, because I collapsed mid-vision and fell beyond the protective shield. Azazel can feel the Oracles outside the shield! He now knows there are two of us in here!"

I took a deep breath, trying to go over what I'd just explained, hoping that I'd made enough sense for him to understand why I was so horrified.

On top of it all, I still couldn't understand how I'd gotten so close to the boundary. I thought I'd kept a safe distance from it. How had I fallen in the first place? I wasn't sure whether it was the Nevertide Oracle's fault or whether I'd simply lost a couple of feet during the vision.

Bijarki held me steady as I leaned into him. My knees felt weak.

"I won't let anything happen to you, Vita. I've said it before, and I'll say it again." His voice was low and husky, rippling through me.

Hot tears streamed down my cheeks as his expression shifted from concerned to pained. He held me in his arms so close that I could feel his heartbeat.

"I can't stand the sight of you crying," he said, then lowered his head and captured my mouth in a sweet kiss.

The fears I'd harbored began to flutter away like dry leaves in the wind, as I allowed myself the luxury of being comforted by Bijarki. He didn't hold back as an incubus anymore. His effect washed over me like a hot summer breeze. I abandoned myself in his arms as he pressed further, his tongue invading and tasting, his lips a perfect fit for mine.

My breathing was labored and broken, my body unable to control itself anymore. My head felt light, and, for just one second, everything seemed okay. There was no Azazel. No Destroyers. No one eager to capture or kill us. It was just me and Bijarki, lost in a kiss meant to help me forget everything except him.

He paused to look at me, his silvery eyes searching for something.

"We're in so much trouble," I muttered, once again reminded of the last few minutes of my never-boring existence.

"I've got you, little fae," he whispered, dropping a kiss on the tip of my nose.

Noises outside startled us, making us stand apart. His hand took mine as we headed back outside. I heard Serena's voice and was instantly relieved and thrilled.

They were back.

32

SERENA

We emerged from the grotto, finding the mansion bathed in orange light, a typical Eritopian sunset that I'd grown fond of. Relief made my feet feel light as I crossed the lawn and reached the porch steps, calling out Phoenix, Aida, and Vita's names.

Draven, Hansa, Sverik, and Jax soon joined me. The rest of our group came out of the house. Vita and Aida squealed as they jumped over the porch. They grabbed me in a long and affectionate embrace, kissing my face and hair.

"It's so good to see you!" Aida said.

"And we have so, so much to tell you," Vita added, visibly concerned.

My instinct kicked in then, warning me that we were in for some not-too-good news. Anjani came out next, hugging her sister. Jovi, Bijarki, Field, and Phoenix slipped out behind them.

My brother hurried over to hug me, holding me tight and exhaling sharply. I felt his arms shake a little, and I understood then just how worried he'd been and how happy he was to see me again.

"I told you I'd make it back in one piece," I quipped, well aware of my pre-departure pessimism. I was genuinely blissful to hold my brother close after the passage stone journey.

Tamara and Eva came out of the mansion as well, followed by two young succubi. I recognized the smudges of red war paint and their leather garments as elements of the Red Tribe, and I looked at Anjani, who nodded at me while beaming a bright white smile.

"They made it?" I managed to ask just as Jovi and Field hugged me at the same time. I laughed.

"They did! But they went out to rally more rebels," Anjani replied. "I'll explain later. It's good to see you!"

"I see the little ones stayed behind!" Hansa practically squealed with delight and opened her arms wide, falling to one knee.

The succubi ran down the steps and jumped on her. Their skinny arms wrapped around her as they hugged her tightly. Hansa's eyes filled with tears as she held them close, kissing their cheeks over and over again.

"The Daughters have been kind and spared your lives," she said to them. "I'm humbled and fortunate to be able to hold you in my arms now."

"We've missed you, Hansa," one of them muttered, hiding her face in Hansa's black mane.

"I've missed you too, my darlings." Hansa sniffed and stood up, letting the girls stand by her side as she wiped her tears with the back of her hand.

"I cannot explain how good it is to see all of you!" I exclaimed, smiling at everyone.

It took us a few minutes to say our hellos and for Draven to introduce Jaxxon, Lord of the Maras, to our group. Jax measured each of us carefully, squinting at the sight of Aida, Vita, and Phoenix, before he looked at me again. He nodded toward my brother.

"Sentry?" he asked.

"And Oracle," I replied.

"Ah. Double trouble, then," Jax remarked. He quickly glanced around, frowning at the sight of Destroyers and green fireflies still moving around the protective shield. "I'm not sure you noticed, but there are Destroyers out there trying to get in."

"Like I've said before. They cannot get in," Draven said, watching Goren as he prowled around, still searching for weak spots.

Jax stilled as the Daughter came out of the house, her reddish pink hair loose around her shoulders. She moved to Phoenix's side, holding his arm and slowly leaning into him. My brother gave her a quick, affectionate glance before he focused his attention back on the Mara.

The Daughter's eyes were a most peculiar violet, making Jax

narrow his own eyes as he tried to figure out what she was. His face dropped once he realized.

"Looks like a goddess," he murmured, then looked at me. "A Daughter of Eritopia? Really? Is this what you meant when you said you had the Daughters' support?"

"Pretty much, yes."

"I understand now why you were ready to kill me if I came all the way here and decided not to join your alliance. I would've done the same," he said, filled with awe, then bowed respectfully before the Daughter, whose confused expression was downright adorable. "It is an honor to meet you, Daughter of Eritopia."

She didn't seem to know how to react and looked around at us for clues. Phoenix gave her a gentle nudge and a smile, nodding toward Jax.

"There you go. I told you your kind is famous around here," he joked, making her giggle.

Vita stepped forward, beads of sweat gathered on her forehead. It was only when I got a second look at her that I realized exactly how pale she was.

"Vita, what's wrong?" I asked.

She gave me a weak smile. "We all need to talk. A lot of things have happened while you've been gone."

We gathered in the banquet hall. Phoenix stood tall, while the rest of us took our seats. A plethora of dishes appeared on the serving plates, prompting Jax to raise an eyebrow.

"Ancient ward magic," I said briefly.

"Okay, I'll go first, to maintain a chronology, so we don't miss anything along the way," Phoenix started. "First of all, a strange thing happened."

"Of the many normal things that have been occurring since we got here?" Jovi smirked, pouring himself a glass of water.

"Aida, Vita, and I got together for a session," Phoenix continued. "But this time, we only had one vision each."

"After which, later on, I had a set of three by myself," Aida added.

"That's strange," Draven seemed intrigued. "Please, go on."

Phoenix continued. "I was somewhere in the distant past, during Azazel's first expansion campaign, when he took over Almus's kingdom. Ten young Druids were helped to escape just as Destroyers came after them. The elder Druids stayed behind to stall them, so the young Druids could make it out of there alive. They flew away on winged horses. This happened at a massive temple. I believe it was the Grand Temple you mentioned, where young Druids were taught the magical arts."

"Did you register any names? The elders, maybe?" Draven asked, his interest piqued. He sat up straight, his elbows on the table.

"Yes. First of all, Goren was one of the Destroyers sent to get the young Druids. Second, one of the elder Druids' names was Drago. The Druids called him Master."

"Drago was one of the principals of the Grand Temple. He taught my father and mother when they first joined. I heard he died during the invasion, along with the students," Draven mused.

"He did die. But I don't think the students suffered the same fate," Phoenix replied. "They were told the horses would take them to the shelter and that Jasmine would wait for them there. Do you know who Jasmine is?"

Draven nodded. "Jasmine was my father's younger sister. This is extraordinary." He stood up and paced around the table. I could sense his excitement, the weary joy of learning that there might still be other Druids out there—and family at that!

"If those Druids survived," he added, "we need to find them. Aida, you should focus on them for your next visions. If they're alive, an Oracle will be able to see them."

"Speaking of Druids and present days," Aida replied, "I saw Patrik during my first vision. He's struggling with Azazel's darkness controlling him. He's pushing back. It's incredibly painful from what I could tell, but he's actually trying to resist and shift back. I saw him myself. His eyes shifted back to their original color, and his bones crackled. But Azazel's hold is still very strong. I'm surprised he made it that far in his attempts to reverse it."

"I thought once you said yes to Azazel, once his darkness took over, you could no longer go back," I replied, confused.

"Technically speaking, you can't," Draven said. "But one should never underestimate the strength of one's will. Or the power of one's emotions. They might shatter the most impenetrable of spells."

He glanced at me as he said that, giving me the impression of something deeper lying beneath his words. Something he'd aimed specifically at me. My heart skipped a beat. I felt like this was his way of telling me that no matter what came at us, our feelings for each other were strong enough to help us overcome it all.

"It would be interesting to see him," he added, shifting his focus back on Aida.

"Who? Patrik?"

He nodded. "I wonder how much self-control he has, given his condition. What his reaction would be at the sight of me. After all, he was loyal to my parents. He would have died for them. Which is why I still don't understand how he wound up saying yes to Azazel instead." He sighed.

"Oh, I can answer that," Aida replied. "After our Oracle session together, I went up on the roof and somehow ended up having another set of visions. In the first one, I was in the company of Destroyers just outside the shield. They were commenting about Azazel. Most of them don't like him but have no choice but to follow, given his control over them. They think he's too proud and weak, despite his magical prowess."

"Weak? How so?" Draven asked.

I watched the expressions around the table, as Aida explained what she'd heard.

"They say he's still pining over Tamara and that he's

desperate to find her. According to his self-professed hate of Lamias, he might be looking to kill her and her daughter, who is considered an abomination."

Tamara scoffed, placing her hand on top of Eva's and giving her a warm, reassuring look. Eva wore a weak smile in return and glanced at Draven, lust flaring in her yellow eyes. I felt the urge to throw a glass pitcher at her head but decided instead to look away and take a deep breath for the sake of our alliance.

"The Destroyers think that Azazel just wants Tamara back. After Genevieve refused his advances, he started losing his mind bit by bit. Despite his violent treatment of Tamara, they say he still longs for her. I'm telling you, Druid, the Destroyers may be following orders because they have no other choice, but I have a feeling that if they're given the opportunity of a cure against Azazel's dark magic, they might take it."

"Duly noted," he replied, then looked at me. "We'll look into this."

I nodded.

"Now, back to Patrik, to answer your question," Aida said, then looked at Tamara. "You're going to want to pay attention to this one. I saw your sister, Kyana."

The Lamias instantly straightened their backs. Their eyes were wide, and their lips parted with shock. Tamara's hand gripped Eva's.

"She's alive?" Tamara gasped.

"Patrik's looking after her. Sort of," Aida replied. "She's a prisoner in Azazel's dungeon. Patrik keeps trying to find out where you are. Obviously, Kyana's not telling him anything, even though he insists he just wants to warn you."

"Warn me of what?"

"That Azazel is intensifying his search for you," Aida said, then looked at Draven and me. "Point is, Patrik and Kyana used to be together before he was turned. He loves her, and something tells me she still loves him too. I saw her cry after he left. But given his condition, not much can happen between them. One thing is for sure, though. The only reason why Patrik said yes to Azazel instead of choosing death was because of Kyana. Her life was at stake. If he hadn't said yes, she would have been killed. Patrik chose to become a monster to keep her alive."

"Wow. There is so much to work with, here," I said, going over all possible scenarios involving Patrik.

As disgusting and ferocious as the Destroyers were, Aida's insights shed a light on who they really were and how they were dealing with what had happened to them. It made me wonder about the others. If Patrik had chosen to say yes because he wanted to protect Kyana, what leverage had Azazel had on the rest of the Destroyers? How many of them, besides Goren, had accepted his darkness willingly?

"And last, but not least," Aida breathed out. "The nasty part of this Oracle business, of which I am unwillingly a part of. My third vision took me to the top of Azazel's castle, where he keeps his Oracles. I saw three in his possession. Two are apparently comatose and unresponsive. The third is the Nevertide Oracle. She saw me in the vision. She could see me there, in front of her, in real time. She tried to warn me—or at least that's what she said. She told me there's a traitor among us and that we're not safe."

We all looked at each other. A whiff of suspicion hung in the air.

My stomach churned as an uncomfortable heat seeped into me. It was doubt, and I wasn't sure which of us to aim it at. None of us had any reason to betray the alliance. On the contrary; we all wanted Azazel dead and Eritopia free.

"She previously told Vita it doesn't have to be a conscious act," Aida continued, "that Azazel's spell didn't require one's consciousness to get results, which is even worse, because if that's true, it means any one of us could be susceptible to his darkness."

A moment passed in silence before she let out another heavy breath.

"He saw me," Aida said.

All eyes were on her, popping out of our sockets. I froze, unable to move or react.

"I was standing right there in the vision, in front of the Nevertide Oracle, when Azazel popped out of nowhere and said, 'Gotcha!' like he'd caught a mouse or something. I woke up screaming, still here. I think he knows about me now."

"Did he look at you, specifically?" Draven asked.

"Yes."

He ran a hand through his hair, mulling over everything he'd just been told. I paid close attention to the emotions he experienced through the channel open between us. I felt genuine concern and a sliver of fear as he looked at me. His steely eyes flickered black for a second before he blinked and glanced at Vita.

"My turn," she said.

"And what good news do you bring?" he asked her, sarcasm dripping from his voice.

I couldn't blame him for feeling what he did. We'd gotten to the point where I was afraid to ask how all this could possibly get worse. Vita looked down.

Bijarki sat next to her and watched her carefully.

"I was on top of Azazel's castle again. I know what that bright pink flash was now," she said slowly. "It was the Daughter, sacrificing herself to destroy Azazel. It turns out that a Daughter's touch can no longer kill Azazel. That's how powerful he's become. So she unleashes all that energy inside of her and wipes us all out in the process. I got to see everything from my previous vision from a different angle. We're all up there. Draven is badly wounded." She gave me a pained look. "Aida, Field, Jovi, Phoenix, you, Bijarki... We're up there with Azazel when the Daughter appears out of nowhere. It all ends there in a bright pink flash."

She shuddered as Bijarki took her hand and held it tight, helping her regain her composure.

I felt my eyes sting. Tears rushed to the surface. I swallowed them all back, battling a wave of grief and disappointment. I had to keep it together for the sake of our entire group and our survival. Draven came to stand next to my chair, placing a hand on my shoulder and squeezing gently, as if trying to comfort me. I realized then that I, too, was projecting some very intense emotions that he'd learned to pick up on.

"Azazel has a Daughter in his possession," she added.

"What?" Draven asked, stunned.

We were all stunned.

"He snatched an egg off Mount Agrith and forced it to hatch before its time. He refers to her as the little one, and he's holding her as leverage against the Daughters," Vita continued.

"It's true," the Daughter interjected. "I spoke to my sisters in a dream. I told them I want nothing to do with this. I told them I don't want to kill you all. I only want peace and Azazel gone. And I asked them about our sister. They said he draws enormous amounts of power from her, not just from the volcanoes. It's why a Daughter's touch can no longer kill him."

"Then why did they ask me to protect you?" Draven asked, gritting his teeth.

Anger blazed from him, red and intense. He felt betrayed by the Daughters, and I couldn't disagree. Not after everything he'd been through.

"Because my egg came after our sister was taken," the Daughter said. "Eritopia reacted to Azazel by giving birth to her, but he was cunning and fast and took her away. He made a deal with my sisters. They don't intervene in his expansion plans, and he makes sure she stays alive. Because she was hatched so early, she's very vulnerable. Everything they did for you was part of a loophole in the deal. Even the way they isolated Eritopia from the rest of the universe was their way of limiting his power without breaking the terms of their arrangement."

"Something else happened." Vita's voice was weak. "Just before you got here. I was outside, by the shield, when the Nevertide Oracle reached out to me as well. I had a strange vision of her. Well, through her, sort of. Apparently, there's one thing about the Oracles that Azazel doesn't know, that no one knows. We can communicate with each other directly, through some form of projection, outside of visions. We can look into each other's souls and see the truth of our visions, although I'm not yet sure how to do that on my own. Thing is, I fainted and fell through the shield."

She broke down crying, no longer able to hold it in. Bijarki wrapped an arm around her, pulling her close to him, and looked up at us.

"She got back just in time, but Goren saw her. And Azazel most likely sensed her presence as soon as she fell through the shield," Bijarki said.

Draven groaned and let his head fall back, eyes rolling. My heart ached for him, for myself, for all of us. It felt like with each step we took forward, something pulled us two steps back. Every inch of progress came at a very high and painful cost.

It took us a few minutes to digest everything and accept the fact that Azazel knew for a fact that there were Oracles beneath the protective shield.

"He'll want to come here himself," Draven said.

"Would that be such a bad thing?" Jax interjected, his tone low and cool.

"Not if you enjoy having your entrails ripped out through your mouth," Sverik shot back sarcastically.

"No, wait," Draven replied. "The Mara has a point. There is an upside to this entire situation. Azazel would be the one to come to us. We wouldn't have to venture out to his castle and engage in a full-on siege. He'd be on our turf. We'd have better control of the fight here and perhaps a better shot of killing him directly, provided we get some inside help."

"Inside help?" Hansa asked.

"Someone who could give us some of his weak points in a setting such as this, who could help us level the playing field without anyone else knowing," Draven explained. "We're due to meet and establish the alliance with the rogue nations in six moons' time. We could bring them here from Mount Agrith to defend the shield and draw Azazel out here. He'll be intrigued to see rogues defending the Oracles hidden beneath. He'll be curious enough once he realizes he cannot breach the protective shield, even if he's getting power from the Daughter. He would've done it by now if he could."

"Okay, let's say that works, and we draw him out, and we get the alliance to fight and defend us," Hansa replied. "Who would you have on the inside to tip the scales in our favor?"

"Someone he thinks he has under complete control and has trusted with a significantly large army, plus the keys to his dungeons," Draven replied steadily, then gave me a sideways glance.

It dawned on me who he had in mind. We said his name at the same time:

"Patrik."

33

SERENA

An hour later, we were still in the banquet hall going over all possible outcomes. We'd managed to get past the initial shock and fear of these new developments and focus instead on what should come next.

"We need to hold out for six more days," Draven said, with newfound strength. "On the seventh day, we'll use whatever small amount of ingredients we have left for the invisibility spell to sneak out to Mount Agrith. Then we'll bring the garrisons here and take our unwanted neighbors by surprise. I reckon Azazel will want to come here himself by then."

"How sure are you that this protective shield can resist his Daughter-powered magic, though?" Jax replied.

"The shield is meant to protect me," the Daughter spoke up. "My sisters will not sacrifice me for the stolen Daughter. They will not get involved in any way, and the shield will hold as long as I'm inside."

Jax nodded slowly, occasionally glancing around the table, as if analyzing each of us carefully.

"What about the traitor, then?" he asked.

"We don't know for sure there is a traitor. The Nevertide Oracle cannot be trusted," Vita said, and Aida nodded her agreement.

"She told both me and Vita that there's a traitor in our group, but in both moments of contact, she screwed us big time. I was seen by Azazel, and Vita fell through the shield, enough for Goren to see her and the dark overlord to feel her. Frankly, I don't trust her one bit," Aida added.

"Nevertheless, it should still be considered as a risk." Jax cocked his head to one side.

"We're not rejecting the idea. We just don't know where to start or how to ascertain which one of us could be under his spell." I stood up, feeling the need to move. I felt restless and irritated as I paced around the hall.

"So, for now, we just have to get used to Destroyers lurking outside," Jovi muttered, leaning back into his chair. He gave Anjani a sideways glance, and in return she offered him a half-smile. The succubus brought her hand up to her chest, fingers fiddling with a small pendant I'd not seen before—a wolf's head holding a diamond between its fangs.

"Sure," Phoenix chimed in. "Might as well bring them

breakfast every morning, don't you think? I don't think Azazel feeds them well."

Jax smirked, his attention set on my brother.

The Mara joined the boys' banter. "I don't think they like the cooked stuff much."

"At least coffee," Phoenix mumbled, prompting Jovi to laugh and slap him over the shoulder.

Jax then looked at me, his jade eyes smiling.

"I like your brother. He's got spunk," he said, his voice low as Phoenix and Jovi continued to crack jokes at the Destroyers' expense in the background, making the girls smile and easing some of the tension weighing heavy on our shoulders.

"Yes, they're both out of this world," Draven interjected, his gaze finding mine.

The double entendre was an absolute hit with my senses, making me smile for a moment. I was fortunate to have him near me, his strength and golden energy fueling me even when I thought I didn't need it. I fought the urge to hold him and kiss him right then and there. I poured myself a glass of water, crisp and cool, courtesy of the wards.

I noticed Eva staring at Draven from the other side of the table, one finger running along the rim of her glass as she measured him from head to toe. I felt irritation simmer inside me. I watched her persistently until she looked at me.

As soon as our eyes met, I raised an eyebrow. She rolled her eyes at me, then resumed gawking at Draven. I scoffed, looking forward to the day I'd see the back of her as she wandered back to the River Pyros.

Draven gave me a nudge with his elbow, humor flickering in his steely eyes.

"Don't be mad, Serena," he whispered. "Consider it fate repaying you for Zeriel and his obnoxious ogling. Jealousy can be a cruel mistress."

"I'm not jealous of her, Druid. I know who makes you all soft and gooey on the inside, and it's not a spoiled Lamia. I just don't like her," I shot back with a smirk.

His eyes went black for a split second, before he licked his lips and smiled.

"Hey Draven!" Aida called from her seat.

He turned to face her, breaking eye contact and leaving me with a smoldering heat in my chest. I looked forward to another moment alone with him. The two of us had a lot to catch up on, and the thought sent my pulse racing.

"What shall we focus on next, as far as visions go?" Aida asked.

"You should certainly keep an eye on Patrik and Azazel. Their next moves are very important, as we may need Kyana to sway Patrik back on the right track. You could also see if the young Druids survived," Draven replied.

"You're up for another trip to Luceria, then?" Hansa quipped, half-smiling.

"If it helps bring Azazel to his knees, might as well," he replied.

"Looking forward to experiencing another one of his death stares?" I shot back, reminding him of how he'd nearly drowned during our escape down the river because of his eye contact with Azazel.

"Not if it can be avoided."

"I'll continue to check the future for changes," Vita intervened, her eyebrows drawn into a frown. "With everything that's happened over the past twenty-four hours, chances are we've influenced the outcome."

"Agreed." Draven nodded, then looked at Phoenix. "Can you focus on the young Druids in the meantime? We need to find out where they went and whether they found Jasmine. We need the full story before we start looking for them in the present."

"Sure," my brother said. "I'm extremely curious myself."

The Daughter caught my eye. Her head rested on Phoenix's shoulder. She looked lost and sad.

"What's wrong?" I asked her gently.

"I don't want to blow up," she replied. Her voice faded. "My sisters say that my sacrifice will be required no matter what we do. But I don't want to hurt any of you. I can't."

"Listen to me, because I'm only going to say this once." I took a deep breath. "As long as there are Shadians around you, you will not perish, and you will not hurt us. We will do everything in our power to make sure we all come out in one piece. The only one who gets obliterated will be Azazel."

Phoenix beamed at me, proud and bold, as he held the Daughter's hand in his. I believed in everything I'd just said, even though our circumstances made it difficult. But I knew, deep in my heart, that as long as I kept my resolve strong and unyielding, there was nothing I couldn't do. And if we were all of the same mindset and on the same wavelength, we could become a truly unstoppable force.

34

VITA

By nightfall, we'd all retired to our rooms, utterly exhausted. I shared a bed with Aida and Serena again. We did our own personal catching up.

We'd been through plenty of horrors, but we'd also been experiencing some truly amazing things. Who did I share these moments with, if not my best friends?

However, before the strike of midnight, Aida and Serena were both asleep. My mind raced in one too many directions, and the humid heat wasn't helping either. I tossed and turned, once again thinking about the visions I'd had and the concept of a traitor among us. Was the Nevertide Oracle telling the truth, or was it just a ruse? Who could it be? Would they even be aware of it?

I looked out the window and let out a heavy sigh. The sky was a perfect giant tourmaline sprinkled with stars and crowned with a giant pearl for a moon that cast its milky light into our room. I wasn't going to fall asleep anytime soon.

I got out of bed and tiptoed into the open corridor, making my way to the upstairs study. I figured I could read something to put myself to sleep.

I passed by one of the remaining spare bedrooms and spotted a figure at the corner of my eye, stopping me in my tracks. I turned my head to get a better look and saw Bijarki standing by the open window. The night breeze rolled in, lifting the fine off-white organza curtains. He looked breathtaking under the moonlight, his skin shimmering silver as he gazed outside.

He sensed my presence in the doorway and turned to look at me, his eyes scanning me briefly before darkening. I felt over-exposed all of a sudden. My cheeks flushed as I realized I was wearing one of the skimpier undergarments I'd found in the attic, a short summery gown with shoulder straps that left much of my skin bare.

"What are you doing here?" I asked in a hushed tone.

"Just doing my part to try and prevent that awful future from happening." He shrugged, unable to look away. "You said we'd be in my room when the Destroyers came in, so I figured I'd move here for a while. Not sure how much that helps, but it beats doing nothing."

His voice was low and pained, compelling me to take a few steps forward and get a better look at his face. He wore his emotions raw, and it tore me apart on the inside. I couldn't stand seeing him like this and cursed my Oracle abilities for casting such dark shadows on our budding relationship.

His torment was my misery. I felt tears welling in my eyes. He stilled as I wiped them off quickly, his hand reaching into his pocket. He swallowed, then came toward me, stopping when there were only a couple of inches left between us.

He raised his hand to show me a small pendant with a perfectly polished turquoise stone attached to a delicate silver chain. It hung from two fingers.

"Jovi got a special pendant for Anjani from an old fae in the Sarang Marketplace," he murmured. "This one isn't of any mystical quality, but I found it to be a perfect complement to your eyes. I figured it would look beautiful on you."

I lost my ability to speak for a moment. My gaze fixed to the little stone dangling before me. My lips parted, and I tried to figure out if I was still breathing. He looked at me, waiting for a reaction.

"It's beautiful," I whispered.

Our eyes met, his smiling gently.

"Can I put it on you?" he asked.

I nodded.

His hands reached around the back of my neck as I lifted my hair in a careless handheld bun. His fingers brushed my skin as they clasped the silver chain in place, sending shivers down my spine. His fingers followed the chain to the front, moving slowly past my collarbones to touch the turquoise stone.

My breathing staggered as a familiar warmth spread

through my body. His silvery eyes kept me still. He frowned, a muscle jumping in his lower jaw as he lowered his head.

I gazed up at him towering in front of me.

"It looks beautiful," he said. "But it's nothing without you. It's just a stone."

I smiled as my hand reached his face, touching his cheek. His body heat seeped through me, and he leaned into my touch, closing his eyes to enjoy the moment. When he opened them, I felt the full force of his incubus nature unwinding, enveloping me in smooth threads of desire and something else, something far more profound and not so easy for me to understand.

My head felt light as he took a small step forward and completely closed the distance between us. I inhaled deeply in response, unable to utter a word.

"You'll have to forgive me, Vita," he whispered, "but I can't take it anymore."

His incubus nature continued amplifying its effect on me. I felt myself on the verge of unraveling into millions of particles. My tongue moved slowly over my lower lip, and I swallowed back the last of my reserve regarding intimacy with him.

"Forgive what, Bijarki, when I can barely hold my own whenever I'm close to you?"

His gaze softened as his mouth possessed mine, taking me away from the palpable and throwing me into a whirlpool of delightful chills and addictive heatwaves. His hands moved up as he held my face and deepened the kiss, his tongue working mine with masterful precision.

I knew, right then and there, that he would be my future and my very undoing—and there was no other way I would've wanted it. I wrapped my arms around his neck and lifted myself on my toes, leaning into him.

I was tender against him, and his strong muscles felt as though they'd been carved in marble. My pulse thudded through my veins, sending waves of hot and cold at the same time, confusing my senses and throwing me even closer to the edge. His fingers traveled slowly down my neckline and shoulders and settled on the small of my back.

His kiss turned hungry. His teeth grazed my lower lip as he slowly lifted me off the ground. I felt weightless as he turned us around, shutting the bedroom door with his foot and setting me on the bed in front of him without parting his lips from mine. His breathing was erratic as his mouth moved down my chin, licking and nipping his way down to my shoulder.

It was so right, so perfect. I completely removed myself from reality and prayed to all the gods for Bijarki to be able to feel everything that he was making me feel in this moment and beyond. He stopped for a second to look at me, desire glimmering in his eyes as his fingers brushed one of the straps off my shoulder.

"You are the single most incredible part of my life, Vita, and it's come to a point where I cannot imagine living without you anymore." His husky voice sent tremors directly into my soul.

I touched his lips, losing myself in his gaze and taking the final leap of faith toward him.

"I'm hopelessly in love with you," I whispered.

His eyes opened wide, and a dizzying array of emotions flickered in his irises, of which I was somehow able to recognize the predominant one like a flare in the middle of a pitch-black night.

"Good," he smiled, "because I fell for you the moment I first laid eyes on you, little fae, and it is equal parts terrifying and exhilarating."

He kissed me, this time unleashing the passion that had been brewing between us for days. I allowed myself to fall back on the bed, and Bijarki followed. My core heated up and expanded like a young sun. His body covered mine, and his hands roamed all over, taking in every line and curve they encountered until they reached the hem of my gown.

I responded to his kiss, my fingers digging into his firm shoulders as he lifted the fabric up to my thighs. His touch on my bare skin pushed me so close to the edge, I could feel the earth disappearing from beneath us. He groaned and pulled himself up, looking down at me, his bedroom eyes making my heart flutter in my chest.

He lifted the dress further, and I raised my arms above my head as he removed it completely and threw it on the floor. He didn't move for a while, looking at me and taking all of me in as if admiring a painting. His adoration ignited an uncontrollable blaze in my core, making it impossible for me to control my ragged breathing.

We were utterly in love, gazing at each other under the moonlight.

"I never thought I'd be fortunate enough to have you here with me," he breathed.

I sat up, ready to take this to the next level and hopefully reach the stars with my incubus. He watched quietly as I unbuttoned his shirt. His knuckles moved up and down my arms. I removed the fabric from his broad torso and set him free. His skin perfectly stretched over toned muscles, each delightfully mine to play with.

Bijarki then took me in his arms and pressed me deeper into the bed. I whimpered under his grip. His fingers dug into my flesh, as the tension built to impossible levels. His skin on mine was pure bliss, as we kissed and discovered each other inch by inch, late into the night.

"I'm yours," I managed to say as his mouth claimed my neck, slowly moving down and tasting everything he could before reaching my navel.

I ran my fingers through his hair as he took me higher. We lost ourselves as our bodies and souls demanded that we become one complete being. His hands took mine and stretched my arms upward. I pushed my chest forward. He exhaled sharply and ravaged me with a deep, mind-shattering kiss.

Everything else disappeared. The world dematerialized, atom by atom, as our physical forms fused and our spiritual beings intertwined. I felt him deep in my heart, like a flame burning hotter with each minute. The universe spiraled into nothingness as his voice guided me further away from the edge of reason.

I gasped out his name, and he held me tight as we exploded and dissolved into cosmic stardust. His love rippled through me, and I felt tears streaming down my face, this time tears of sheer joy, a rapture I never thought I'd ever experience, a slice of divinity that I didn't know existed.

"And I am yours," he whispered in my ear.

I looked him in the eyes and kissed him for the millionth time—or more. I'd lost track.

"Good," I breathed, my lips on his.

"Don't let go," he said as he took me higher, his touch setting wildfires through me that only his mouth was capable of putting out.

He whispered my name over and over, until I felt him surrender and break down, shuddering in my arms as our love blossomed and brought us closer together, beyond the physical realm. His incubus nature amplified everything, making each second seem like an eternity, and we both wanted as many eternities as we could possibly get.

I didn't let go. I couldn't bear to leave him. My skin belonged on his. My heart was locked in his. He held me close for a while, our bodies naked and glistening with pure elation, our souls victims of euphoria.

We weren't ready to come down. We didn't want to. Reality could wait. I was in no rush.

35

AIDA

I'd dozed off for a couple of hours, but opened my eyes when I felt Vita leave and sneak out. That old mattress was not able to keep a secret.

I was staring out the window, enjoying the night sky in its full splendor when a cold wave hit me.

My body froze, my muscles stiff as the world began to spin uncontrollably. Ice cluttered my veins as the image before me dissolved into darkness, and I slipped into a vision.

I stood in Azazel's chamber. I recognized the setting, the polished black marble, the sumptuous furniture, and the disturbing green fires hanging overhead. He was sitting in a tall chair, his elbows on the armrests as his serpent tail twitched.

The gold snake pendant moved incessantly, its ruby eyes spelling nothing but disaster.

My heart jumped in my throat. What if he could see me? I watched him for a while until I decided to try something. I had to make sure this was a regular vision and not another living nightmare.

"Hey, you," I muttered, waiting for a reaction.

He didn't even look my way.

"You're a slimy slithering bastard. Did you know that?"

Still, nothing. Relief washed over me as I confirmed this to be a plain vision. If anyone would have told me a month earlier that I'd worry over the palpability of a vision as a part of my daily routine, I would have slapped them silly. And yet, I was pleased to have the certainty that he couldn't see, hear, or even feel me. I had a lot to tell him.

"You are an embarrassment to your entire species," I said, gritting my teeth. "You're an embarrassment to the entire planet. Nope, the galaxy. Nope. Let's go with the whole universe. You are sick. You are twisted. You're a frustrated garden variety snake who somehow got his filthy little tail wrapped around way too much mojo and decided he was better than everyone else. I root for the day you finally drop to the floor, lifeless. And I don't say this lightly. I've never wished death upon anyone but you. You! You should really just drop dead."

I took a few steps forward, emboldened by my own anger.

"Just. Die," I added. "Die. Right now. Drop dead. Come on, you can do it. Just stop breathing. Die!"

The doors opened behind me, startling me. I squealed and jumped back a couple of feet, as two Destroyers slithered in, carrying a massive passage stone. Green fires threw reflections off its obsidian surface. They struggled with it until they managed to put it down without tipping it over.

"Careful," Azazel barked. "Many succubi died for this to be here."

He grinned as he said that and stood up, bringing himself closer to it.

As his fingers touched it, sliding down slowly, I broke into a cold sweat. I knew where that stone had come from.

"Get Patrik and four others and bring them to me. I have an errand for them," he hissed.

Everything went dark before I could hear anything else. I cursed under my breath as I slipped away into another vision. My Oracle abilities were still just as surprising as they were infuriating.

I was back in the dungeons, right in front of Kyana's cage. I looked around nervously, certain that I would see Patrik soon enough. These visions had started to follow a predictable pattern, based on what I wanted to see and on the urgency of each event occurring in the present.

This is a completely unexpected session, so it must be important.

Kyana sat up at the sound of metallic noises echoing from the corridor. I saw Patrik come in, a gloomy expression on his face. Their eyes met for a moment, before Kyana scoffed and looked away.

"I can't even bear to look at you," she muttered.

He stopped in front of her, his fingers wrapped around the black iron bars. I could hear sniffing and moaning nearby, as some of the captive creatures cried out in the dark.

"Azazel has summoned me," Patrik replied.

"And?" she shot him a vicious glance.

"And there's a chance I may not return. We're not sure what's waiting at our destination. I came to say goodbye, just in case."

She took a deep breath and fiddled with a lock of her matted, platinum hair. Her golden yellow eyes flickered black for a second, and she looked away.

"Best of luck to you. Snake."

"Kyana," Patrik brought his face closer to her cage. "Everything I have ever done, it was for you. You, and you alone. Hate me all you want, but I sold my soul to the devil so you could live."

She didn't reply, but I could see her frowning as her lower lip trembled.

"If I could, I would let you out this very instant. I would take you far away where no one could ever hurt you, Kyana. But I cannot. My body, my will, they're not mine just yet. Every time my fingers reach for the lock, the pain becomes unbearable. I am trying, though. I am working on making myself stronger. And one day, I will be strong enough to set you free."

She gave him a sideways glance, blinking several times.

"Is this your farewell?" she asked, faking indifference even though the vein pulsing in her temple told me she was anything but indifferent.

"It could very well be," Patrik replied. "And if it is, if this is the last time I see you, Kyana, I want you to know that I love you. I have never stopped loving you. And when I die, I will die loving you."

His hand reached out to her between the bars, his knuckles gently brushing against her cheek. She stilled as he caressed her face for a few seconds. He cautiously withdrew his hand and slithered out of the dungeon.

Kyana watched him disappear in the darkness of the corridor leading upstairs. When silence returned, she shuddered and burst into tears again. My heart felt like breaking once more at the sight of a creature tormented by love, grief, and captivity. I could only imagine how she felt, and I had absolutely no intention of experiencing any of these emotions in the near future.

A sense of urgency came over me as I wondered if Patrik was on his way to meet Azazel.

―――――――――

My third vision anticipated that very question. I found myself standing in Azazel's chamber again. This time, he was in the company of five Destroyers, including Patrik, who'd just come through the giant double doors.

Azazel clapped his hands, rubbing his palms with excitement. His grin turned my stomach upside down.

"Everyone ready?" he asked.

The Destroyers nodded, including Patrik, who glared at the passage stone.

"What are we waiting for?" he replied.

"Your tour guide."

Azazel's reply chilled me to the bone, as the Oracle's warnings suddenly came back, playing in a loop in my head. The passage stone could lead to the mansion if someone knew where our stone was beneath it. My heart went on a frantic rampage in my chest, as the obsidian surface began to ripple on its own.

No.

They all watched it quietly, waiting for someone to come out from the other side.

Oh, no.

A figure walked through the liquid black stone, and my knees nearly gave out as I recognized the Destroyers' tour guide. The traitor. Shock and horror slammed into me.

"Come on. It's time," Sverik said, standing before Azazel with a grim look on his face.

"Excellent," Azazel replied, then slapped Patrik on the back. "Go on! Go fetch me some Oracles!"

Patrik nodded slowly and placed his hand on Sverik's shoulder. The other Destroyers followed suit. They disappeared inside the passage stone, and I reached a hand out to stop them. But I was just a living ghost visiting the present. I could do nothing.

Sverik was the traitor, and, from what I could tell, he was willing. No green flickers, no forced behavior. It was all him.

No.

As the stone resumed its cool black surface, my breathing intensified. Heat shot through my temples.

"I have to warn them," I gasped. "I have to wake up. I have to warn them."

I shook my head, trying to will myself back to consciousness, but nothing happened. I jumped around and shook my arms, then pinched myself repeatedly, but still, nothing. I was still there, standing next to Azazel in front of the passage stone, while Sverik and the Destroyers were most likely slithering into the mansion.

Panic took over as I paced around the chamber, cursing under my breath and slapping myself in a desperate attempt to wake up. When that didn't work, I tried pinching again.

"Damn it," I gasped. "Come on, wake up! Wake up! Wake up, Aida! Wake the hell up!"

"It's annoying when the visions don't listen to you, isn't it?"

Azazel's voice echoed toward me, stunning me.

I stopped breathing, my eyes close to jumping out completely. I stared at him. He shifted his gaze from the passage stone to me, his eyes flaring that wretched green I'd grown too familiar with.

He was looking right at me.

Not through me. Not past me. Right. At. Me.

A second passed, then another, and another. I didn't flinch.

"Why are you in such a rush to leave me, little Oracle?"

36

VITA

We were inseparable, our bodies molded perfectly to one another, hidden beneath the sheets. Neither of us wanted to fall asleep. We prolonged our bliss for as long as possible. His sweet whispers echoed in my heart. His declaration of love and his heart echoed in my soul. Why would I ever want this to stop?

Bijarki was the first to drift away after putting a pair of shorts on, his breathing soft and even on my face. I figured I wasn't too far behind, so I quickly slipped back into my nightgown and hid under the cover, cuddling in his arms as he groaned, kissed my temple, and sank deeper into his dream state.

I watched him sleep, taking in his every feature, memorizing every line and sharp edge. I relaxed in the warmth of his body, thinking that maybe, just maybe, we'd be okay. That no one would tear us apart. That we'd live through this till the very end, and we'd ride off into the sunset victoriously one day, just the two of us.

But I couldn't shake that nasty feeling. That lingering chill that something was not right.

My gaze darted around the room, from the open window that allowed the nighttime chill to cool us, to the candle flickering on the dresser. This wasn't the bedroom from which I'd be taken. It was a different room, and yet, my stomach still tightened.

A thud downstairs made me freeze.

Silence followed for what seemed like forever compressed in a handful of seconds.

The wooden door exploded inward, splinters flying every which way.

Destroyers spilled into the room.

I screamed.

Bijarki jumped upright as the vision I'd predicted began to unfold way too quickly. They hadn't come through the window, but the horror was the same.

The Destroyers hissed and threw their spears at Bijarki. He slipped out of the bed and dodged them as best as he could.

I sprang to my feet as two of the monsters came at me, backing me into the corner next to the dresser.

"Bijarki!" I screamed.

I saw him pulling a spear from the wall. Another poisoned spear whizzed past him, leaving a gash on his shoulder. He managed to glance at me, pale as a vampire, before he collapsed on the floor.

"No!" I cried and grabbed the candle from the dresser.

My instincts kicked in. I poured all my energy into that little flame, and it grew larger in front of me, forcing the Destroyers back. I threw a fireball at one of them and immediately focused on generating another.

The affected Destroyer fell backward, flailing and hissing as the fire consumed him. I could smell the burning flesh as I increased the size of my second fireball. The remaining four Destroyers slithered around the room, trying to reach me.

For a moment I thought I stood a chance. I thought I could keep them away for long enough to see my friends charge into the room and kill the monsters that had come for me. My attention got the best of me, as I glanced at Bijarki, hoping that he was just knocked out.

I was petrified of losing him.

I shifted my focus back on the flame and saw a pair of yellow eyes right in front of me. A heavy blow threw my head to the side, followed by a sharp pain.

The world disappeared.

Darkness came over me.

I tried to scream louder.

But my voice was gone.

Bijarki.

37

PHOENIX

Vita's high-pitched scream, followed by thuds and crashing tore me out of my dreams and right into the devastating reality. I didn't have time to think of anything. Her scream sent chills down my spine and left no room for questions. Something was horribly wrong.

I heard the Daughter gasp as she woke up at the same time. I jumped out of bed and ran out, leaving her behind. The shrill coming from the room next to mine beckoned me to move quickly and ignited my senses.

I reached the open corridor and saw the first door ahead on the left completely gone. Shadows moved inside. Glass broke, and bodies thudded on the floor accompanied by hissing.

My instincts kicked in, as I realized what was happening.

The vision had come true.

Before I could take another step forward, a Destroyer came

out in flames, hissing and screaming, his whole body flailing around as he burned to a crisp. He crashed into the wooden balustrade and tumbled down to the ground floor, obliterating the glass table on which he landed. His constant high-pitched shriek grated against my nerves as the fire kept eating him.

I heard doors opening and steps below.

Three more Destroyers came out, baring their fangs at me with their swords raised, the steel blades glinting.

My sentry nature was swift to react. I pushed out a powerful barrier against one of them, while the other two slithered down the corridor in the opposite direction. The monster I hit shook his head and came back at me, hissing.

I pushed out another pulse.

Jax joined me from behind.

I saw his eyes glowing yellow as he used his mind-bending ability on the Destroyer. Sentry mind control didn't seem to work on Eritopian creatures, but I could still whack them with barriers.

I did exactly that, pushing out one after another as fast as I could while Jax continued bombarding the Destroyer with who-knew-what nightmares, forcing him to his knees.

Hansa appeared from below the first-floor corridor, pulling herself up as she grasped the intact parts of the balustrade and jumped at the monster with her large sword raised high. She brought the blade down in a split-second, beheading the Destroyer as she landed on her feet with impressive agility.

She looked at us over her shoulder, her breathing ragged,

her eyes wide, and her entire being thirsting for Destroyer blood. She wasn't holding any of it back, and, as a sentry, I picked up on that.

"Thanks," I said, and she nodded in response, before I turned my head to face Jax. "And thank you."

Rumbling noises downstairs drew us to the edge, where the other two Destroyers had slithered, slamming each door open as if looking for something or someone. I was willing to bet they were looking for Oracles. Serena rushed downstairs and after them, pushing out a barrier strong enough to knock one of them off its tail. The other moved back, kicking down more doors.

Anjani and Jovi hurried out from Draven's study and joined the fight below, taking on Serena's Destroyer from both sides as he stood up, cursing under his breath.

Jovi charged in, knocking it down once more, as the creature's back hit the floor with a crackling thud. Anjani reacted quickly and jumped up the wall, where battle axes were exhibited between stuffed animal heads.

She grabbed one mid-jump and brought it down with all her might. The wide, sharp blade severed the Destroyer's head while it was distracted by Jovi's multiple head punches.

The one who'd been on fire was dead, lying on its back on top of the shattered table, charred beyond recognition as the flames slowly died out.

Field blocked the fourth Destroyer's path before it reached the greenhouse door. The creature raised its sword at him, but

Field was too fast as he darted from one side to the other, circling around and landing sharp punches in the Destroyer's ribs and kidneys.

He then spread his broad wings out and rammed into the Destroyer, aided by his smooth gliding across the parquet. He shoved him into the wall with such force that the wooden panels splintered under the pressure of the creature's body. We all heard the bones breaking in the process.

Field jumped back, leaving room for Draven to mutter something under his breath and eject a blue flame at the Destroyer. The fire ate him up instantly.

Hansa leaped from our side all the way down in front of him and roared as she smashed the sword into his neck. His burning body stilled. His head fell to the floor.

We all shook from the adrenaline, our breaths ragged as we looked at each other, understanding exactly what had happened. I then remembered where I'd seen the Destroyers come from and ran into the room on my left.

Everything was shattered in there, glass shards scattered all over, the windows broken. Spears were stuck in the wall above the bed.

"In here!" I yelled as I heard more noises and voices downstairs—most likely it was the young succubi and the Lamias coming out of hiding.

Jax joined me in the room where we found Bijarki lying on the floor, unconscious. The Daughter held his head in her lap, her expression horrified as she looked at me.

With everything going on I hadn't even seen her go in.

She had one palm on his shoulder, where a wound had quickly begun to fester. Bijarki was pale and dripping with sweat, barely breathing, as the Daughter's touch turned the injury into a phosphorescent pink patch of skin.

"Please live," she begged him, tears rolling down her cheeks. Her hand flared pink, and the flesh sizzled beneath it.

Bijarki opened his eyes, then turned to one side and vomited black poison.

Serena and the others reached us just in time to witness Bijarki's wound close, leaving just a faint scar behind. He gasped and looked around, stricken with terror as he came to his senses.

"Vita," he croaked. "They took her."

PHOENIX

His words shot chills right into my bones as I realized why the windows were broken.

Aida came through, shaking like a leaf. Her hair was wet with sweat, and her skin was pale. Dark rings circled her eyes as she looked at us with sheer horror.

"I couldn't get out!" she cried. "I had a vision. I saw them use the passage stone. They took Hansa's passage stone and brought it to Azazel's castle!"

She turned around several times, looking for something or someone.

"Sverik! It was Sverik! I saw him! He used our stone to reach Azazel and guided the Destroyers here! They knew exactly where to come and who to come for!"

She stilled, her eyes darting around the room.

"Where's Vita?" she asked.

"Downstairs! The stone!" I cried, realization slamming into me. I ran out without even bothering to take the stairs.

I jumped over the broken balustrade and landed inches away from the burnt Destroyer, then darted through the front door.

The rest of our group followed.

I reached the garden just in time to see a Destroyer carrying Vita's limp body into the grotto, followed by Sverik, who gave us a quick glance.

"Sverik, no!" I shouted after him.

"Sorry, kids. I had no choice." He shrugged and had the audacity to wave goodbye.

"Let go of my cousin, Sverik, or I will tear you apart!" Field's voice boomed as he spread his wings and flew at a low altitude in a desperate attempt to get to Vita in time. He soared over the grass, then rolled as he reached the opening, missing Sverik by a couple of inches as the incubus vanished below.

Draven ran past me, with Serena and Bijarki right behind him. I followed, my heart beating so hard and so fast I could feel it struggling against my ribcage.

"He's moving too fast, I can't mind-bend him!" I heard Jax shout from behind as he came out after us.

We reached the grotto, nearly tumbling down the stone stairs on our way down, but it was too late. The passage stone's surface rippled faintly and returned to its smooth form just as Draven slammed into it. He slapped it several times, anger building up in him.

"Sverik, you bastard!" he bellowed. He turned to face us, breathing heavily, his body shaking with anger. "I will break him," he seethed, punching the wall repeatedly.

Vita was gone, along with Sverik, the traitor.

Rage took over the Druid as he smashed the passage stone to pieces with one stunningly powerful blow. He roared as he fell to his knees, heaving and choking from the dust. Serena stared at him in awe. We all did, wondering where he'd gotten all that strength from, to simply obliterate a massive stone with a single punch.

Aida came to stand next to me, crying.

"I couldn't wake up. I was stuck in Azazel's chamber, and he could see me. He could hear me. He wouldn't let me go. I don't know what he did or how he did it, but he had control over my vision, and he refused to let me wake up. He...he said he'd only let me loose if I passed on his message," she spoke fast, livid and shuddering, swallowing back more tears.

The fact that Azazel could hold her hostage in a vision came with terrifying consequences, making everything that had just happened somehow even worse. It felt like all too much to deal with in this moment, and it would take a while to untangle and translate into something that made sense or that could be resolved.

Serena and I looked at each other, feeling the fear, the anger, and the million other emotions rattling us to our very cores.

Draven stood up, running a bloody hand through his hair as he looked at Aida.

"What did he tell you?" he rasped.

Aida's shoulders dropped, surrendering to another wave of tears.

"He...he said he's coming for us all. H-He said we can't stop him."

A moment passed before Bijarki collapsed on his knees and elbows, groaning and shaking and hiding his face in his palms. I heard him mutter Vita's name over and over. Draven lowered himself next to him and put his hand on his back in a gesture of compassion.

Bijarki was in a lot of pain and none of it physical, as the Daughter had done a surprisingly good job of healing him. He was broken by Vita's abduction, and I could sense his grief, his desperation, his raw pain pouring from him in uncontrollable waves.

"Azazel took Vita," Serena said, staring blankly ahead.

"What do we do?" I asked, my voice barely audible.

The Druid had calmed himself surprisingly quickly. He stood up, swiftly joined by Bijarki. I looked at them, then at the rest of our group. We all looked like hell.

"Azazel clearly knows who's beneath the shield, now," Draven replied. "With Sverik on his side, he has valuable information about our entire mission, including the meeting at Mount Agrith in five days' time."

"He also has Vita now and was able to reach out to Aida through her vision," Serena added.

My stomach churned, as the bigger picture of our situation

began to get clearer with each moment that passed.

"We need to get her back," I said, my whole body still trembling from the adrenaline rush. "We need to warn the others before they travel to Mount Agrith. We need to find out what happened to the young Druids. Maybe they're still alive."

"We need to save Vita," Serena said. Tears glazed her eyes.

Draven put his hand around her shoulder as she took deep breaths, trying to regain her composure. She wiped her eyes and swallowed back another wave of tears.

"The stakes of this bloody game have just been upped," Draven said. "The only thing standing between us and probable death right now is the Daughters' shield. And we don't have a passage stone to sneak out through anymore."

The verdict wasn't encouraging. On the contrary, it was dismal. We had a friend to save and an alliance to protect, a disaster to prevent, and a crazed Prince of Destroyers to defeat. Our lives depended on it.

With Vita gone, we could no longer peek into the future.

With Azazel infiltrating Aida's visions, we couldn't afford to risk the present either—in fact, we had to actively try to figure out a way to stop her from having them.

We only had the past, for the time being—and I wasn't sure if even that was safe. Would Azazel eventually come at me through my visions like he'd done with Aida?

Whatever came after tonight, it was going to be a harrowingly bumpy ride.

But no matter what, we had to get Vita back.

READY FOR THE NEXT PART OF THE NOVAK CLAN'S STORY?

Dear Shaddict,

Thank you for reading *A Passage of Threats*!

The next book, *ASOV 48: A Tip of Balance*, releases **August 19th, 2017**.

Visit: **www.bellaforrest.net** for details.

I look forward to seeing you there.

Love,

Bella xxx

P.S. Join my VIP email list and I'll send you a personal reminder as soon as I have a new book out. Visit here to sign up: **www.forrestbooks.com**

(Your email will be kept 100% private and you can unsubscribe at any time.)

P.P.S. Follow The Shade on Instagram and check out some of the beautiful graphics: @ashadeofvampire

You can also come say hi on Facebook: www.facebook.com/AShadeOfVampire

And Twitter: @ashadeofvampire

NOVAK FAMILY TREE

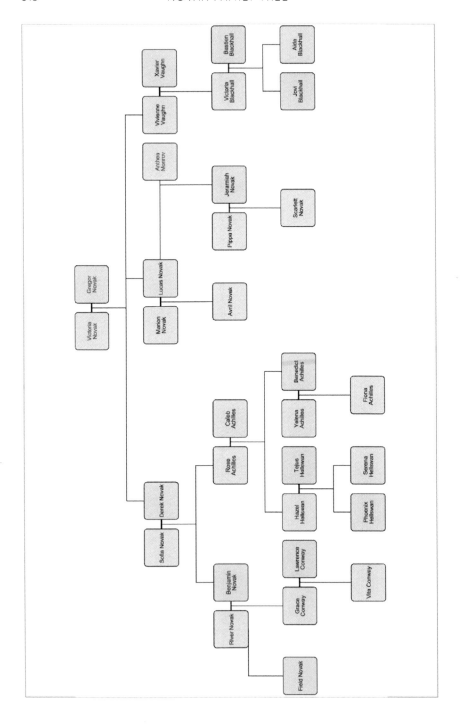

Printed in Poland
by Amazon Fulfillment
Poland Sp. z o.o., Wrocław